PRICE STERN SLOAN
Published by the Penguin Group
Penguin Group (USA) Inc., 375 Hudson Street, New York, New York 10014, USA
Penguin Group (Canada), 90 Eglinton Avenue East, Suite 700, Toronto,
Ontario M4P 2Y3, Canada
(a division of Pearson Penguin Canada Inc.)
Penguin Books Ltd., 80 Strand, London WC2R 0RL, England
Penguin Group Ireland, 25 St. Stephen's Green, Dublin 2, Ireland
(a division of Penguin Books Ltd.)
Penguin Group (Australia), 250 Camberwell Road,
Camberwell, Victoria 3124, Australia
(a division of Pearson Australia Group Pty. Ltd.)
Penguin Books India Pvt. Ltd., 11 Community Centre, Panchsheel Park,
New Delhi—110 017, India
Penguin Group (NZ), 67 Apollo Drive, Rosedale, North Shore 0632, New Zealand
(a division of Pearson New Zealand Ltd.)
Penguin Books (South Africa) (Pty.) Ltd., 24 Sturdee Avenue,
Rosebank, Johannesburg 2196, South Africa

Penguin Books Ltd., Registered Offices:
80 Strand, London WC2R 0RL, England

© 2009 Imagi Crystal Limited / Original Manga © Tezuka Productions Co., Ltd.
Used under license by Penguin Young Readers Group. All rights reserved.
Published by Price Stern Sloan, a division of Penguin Young Readers Group,
345 Hudson Street, New York, New York 10014. *PSS!* is a registered trademark of
Penguin Group (USA) Inc. Printed in the U.S.A.

Library of Congress Control Number: 2009015778

ISBN 978-0-8431-8934-6   10 9 8 7 6 5 4 3 2 1

ASTRO BOY
THE MOVIE

Adapted by Tracey West

IMAGI
STUDIOS

PSS!
PRICE STERN SLOAN

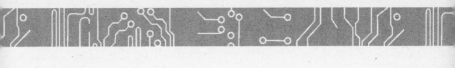

CHAPTER 1

The class full of high school kids yawned in boredom as the lights dimmed. A digital film projected onto a big screen in the front of their classroom.

"The Surface," began the film's narrator. "A desolate wasteland populated by warlike tribes of primitive scavengers. It's survival of the fittest for its unlucky inhabitants." The image of a gleaming metropolis appeared on the screen. "And there we are, Metro City!" The entire city hovered over the Surface of the planet, held up by some unseen force.

Someone in the class groaned. Not another cheesy film about Metro City!

"The jewel in the crown!" boasted the narrator. "Beautiful, isn't it? And all thanks to our friends the robots."

A silver robot wheeled into the scene and began

1

cooking a meal for a family, even reminding the father to call his mom on her birthday.

"That's right! Whether it's serving our meals, raising our children, or building our buildings, no job is too big or too small," the narrator went on. "Including a lot of the things that, frankly, we just don't want to do anymore."

A car whizzed by and dropped a cup on the street. A robot appeared and happily swept up the can. Then . . . *Wham!* A truck whizzed by, running right over the robot. A family appeared looking worried.

"Don't worry! The street will still get cleaned," the narrator promised, as the broken robot was swept into a garbage truck.

The scene cut to a robot factory. Robot workers were making new robots out of parts that sped by on an assembly line.

"You see, robots are not only expendable, they're incredibly cheap to make," the narrator explained. "One robot is created. Then that guy makes himself a new buddy." Now the screen showed a long line of brand-new robots. They marched out of the factory, ready to begin their new jobs.

"Pretty soon all those robots making robots adds up to a whole bunch of robots, eager and willing to serve you and me," the narrator went on. "Thousands are created every day."

"And it's all thanks to this man, Dr. Tenma of the Ministry of Science, also known as the Father of Modern Robotics."

Now the screen showed a tall scientist with a long face, an unruly head of dark hair, and a tuft on his chin to match. He wore a rumpled, white lab coat.

There was a low murmur in the classroom.

"Hey, Toby, isn't that your dad?" a boy asked.

He spoke to the boy sitting next to him. Toby Tenma's black hair was sculpted into shark fin-like points on the top and sides of his head. He was dressed neatly in a blue and red collared shirt and black pants. Toby rolled his wide, brown eyes.

"It sure is," he said, trying to sound like he didn't care. But inside, he was really proud of his father.

Back on the screen, the camera was focused on some children and a robot at a lemonade stand.

"Our friends the robots serve us," the narrator continued. "Thousands are created every day, and thousands are disposed of in the great unending cycle that sustains life in our city."

A garbage truck pulled up filled with old and broken robots. Then the screen showed hundreds of robots being pushed off the side of Metro City. They landed on a great heap of junked robots on the Surface below.

"Thanks for everything, guys," the narrator finished. He chuckled. "May you rust in peace!"

Nobody in the classroom laughed at the joke. The lights in the classroom went on. The teacher, Mr. Moustachio, pressed a button on a remote. The screen went blank. He turned to the room full of kids.

"Okay, students. Pop quiz!" he said cheerfully.

All of the students groaned except for Toby. He actually looked pleased.

Mr. Moustachio passed out the papers. "You have three hours to complete the quiz. Begin."

"I'm so busted!" moaned a girl next to Toby. The rest of the students muttered complaints as they turned over their papers.

Toby didn't hesitate. He entered the answers into his desktop computer at lightning speed. Then he raised his hand.

Mr. Moustachio peered over the book he was reading. "Yes, Toby? Is there a problem?"

"There's no problem," Toby replied. "I'm just finished and I'd like to leave."

The other students gasped.

"Finished?" Mr. Moustachio asked. He looked astonished.

Toby shrugged. "For rocket science, it wasn't exactly rocket science."

"Well, I don't suppose there's much point in you staying—" Mr. Moustachio began, but Toby was already at the door.

He grinned. "Good luck, guys."

He closed the door behind him as the other kids whispered to each other. How could Toby possibly take the quiz so fast?

"Okay, settle down!" Mr. Moustachio ordered.

He checked Toby's answers on his computer. The grade popped up on the screen: 100 percent. The teacher shook his head.

"Just like his father!"

Outside the school, a cheerful house robot waited to greet Toby. Orrin was an early model robot with a fairly simple shape. His head was a round, metal ball with two expressive eyes and a blue laser light for a mouth. His barrel-shaped metal torso was attached to the lower half of his body at the waist by a ball joint, so he could pivot in all directions. Orrin had two arms, but no legs; he rolled around on a single wheel.

Orrin paced back and forth in front of the Tenma limousine. He nervously practiced greeting his master.

"Hello, Master Toby," he began. But that didn't sound right. "No, no, no, no."

He tried again. He had to get it just right. Master Toby could be difficult to please.

"Hello, young sir . . . not young sir, that's . . . Hello! Hello! Hello! Young—how was. How. Hmm . . . "

Toby emerged from the entrance of the school wearing a baseball cap and carrying his schoolbag. Orrin panicked.

"Oh. Oh gosh. Oh my goodness!"

He quickly held the door of the limo open for Toby. "Hello, Master Toby. Uh, good—uh, did you have a good—"

Toby tossed his bag into the air.

"Think fast, Orrin!"

Orrin dove to catch the bag. He grabbed it just before it hit the sidewalk.

"Thank you, Master Toby," Orrin said obediently. "Very good throw, by the way."

Orrin stashed Toby's bag in the limo and took his place in the driver's seat. Toby sat in the backseat. A hologram of his father appeared on the seat next to him.

Dr. Tenma wore his white lab coat, just like in the movie Toby had just seen. His hologram sat stiffly in the seat, and both he and Toby stared straight ahead as they talked.

"Hello, son," Dr. Tenma said.

"Hello, sir," Toby replied.

"How was school?" his father asked.

Toby rolled his eyes. "Oh, great. Moustachio sprung a pop quiz on us, but I'm pretty sure I got a hundred."

"That's good, son. Very good, but I don't want you to become complacent," Dr. Tenma advised. "It's very important to keep studying. Onward and upward, Toby."

"Sure, Dad," Toby said.

Dr. Tenma and Toby cleared their throats at the same time, in exactly the same way. It was easy to see that they were father and son.

"I'm aware that I promised to take you to that symposium on Quantum Mechanics, but I'm afraid I have to take a rain check again," he said.

"I guessed as much," Toby replied. He was disappointed, but he'd never show it.

"I'm sorry, Toby, but it's unavoidable," his father explained. "President Stone has brought forth the unveiling of the Peacekeeper."

"The Peacekeeper? You've got to be kidding me!" Toby cried. He practically bounced in his seat. The Peacekeeper was the largest military robot ever created. He had heard his father talk about it, and he really wanted to see it up close.

"I never kid," Dr. Tenma said seriously. "Good-bye, son."

The hologram disappeared.

"The Peacekeeper, huh?" Toby mused. "Hey, Orrin, change of plan. Take me to the Ministry of Science."

The robot shook his head. "I'm sorry, Master Toby, but your father gave me strict instructions to . . . stop that! Wh-what are you doing back there? Hey! Hey!"

Toby leaned across the seat and quickly worked to rewire Orrin via the control panel on the robot's back. Reprogramming Orrin's orders was child's play.

Orrin stopped protesting. He stepped on the gas.

"Next stop, Ministry of Science."

CHAPTER 2

The sound of marching boots echoed down the gleaming halls of the Ministry of Science. The boots belonged to dozens of soldiers in black uniforms who marched in perfect formation. President Stone, a tall, stern-looking man in black, led the group. He was flanked by Dr. Tenma and his Secretary of Defense, General Heckler.

"Ready to blow me away today, Tenma?" President Stone asked. "To make my hair stand up, to knock my socks off?"

"Er, yes, metaphorically speaking," Dr. Tenma replied. He looked slightly uncomfortable. A man of science, Dr. Tenma preferred calculations and machines to actual people, and President Stone had enough personality for ten men.

"That's the spirit!" Stone said, slapping Dr. Tenma on the back.

"Dr. Elefun is an esteemed colleague of mine, Mr. President," Dr. Tenma began cautiously. "He may be resistant to having his discovery used for military purposes."

"Leave Dr. Elefun to me," President Stone replied darkly.

"Dad!"

Dr. Tenma turned to see Toby running toward them. Orrin followed him, but he was still confused from Toby's rewiring job. The robot kept slamming into the wall.

"Hold that kid! Get him!" one of the soldiers yelled.

A soldier grabbed Toby by his ankle, leaving him dangling upside down. "What are you doing here?" Dr. Tenma said angrily. "I gave Orrin instructions to—"

Orrin slammed into the wall again. "Ow, ow, ow, ow . . ."

"I wanted to see the demonstration," Toby said eagerly. "You're always talking about the Peacekeeper."

"Really, Toby," Dr. Tenma said, annoyed.

President Stone nodded at Toby. "Your boy?" he asked.

"Yes, sir," Dr. Tenma replied.

"Well, let him tag along," President Stone said pleasantly. "It'll be good for him. Educational."

The soldier let go of Toby's leg. "Releasing potential threat," he said.

"So you're interested in robots, son?" President Stone asked. "Robot weapons?"

"Absolutely," Toby answered. "Although I'm sure you'll agree, the latest D-Class Interceptor underlying deployment-to-target systems is quite old-fashioned."

President Stone frowned. "Nobody likes a smarty-pants, kid." He nodded to the soldier. "Take this boy to a safe place and keep him there."

The soldier grabbed Toby again.

"But you said I could see the Peacekeeper!" Toby protested.

"You still can," the president said. "On tonight's news with everybody else."

The soldier dragged Toby away. President Stone and the others marched down the hall and entered a large lecture hall. Rows of metal desks and seats filled with spectators surrounded a round platform. A small, round man in a white lab coat stood on the platform. He had a big, round nose in the center of his pleasant face. He was mostly bald, with a cloud of white hair ringing his head.

"Ladies and gentlemen, allow me to present Blue Core energy," Dr. Elefun said.

A hologram appeared on the stage with him—a giant, glowing sphere of blue light. The crowd gasped in wonder. The light looked soothing and peaceful.

"Blue Core energy," the scientist explained. He stepped closer to the audience. "A new self-sustaining power source much stronger than nuclear energy, and infinitely cleaner."

The hologram changed. A 3-D image of a blue star appeared. The star exploded, breaking into pieces.

"The raw materials came from space," Dr. Elefun went on. "A fragment of a star millions of light years away that no longer even exists. This is now all that's left of it."

The hologram faded, and a light shone on a pillar on the stage. A small, blue globe encased in a glass box sat on top of the pillar.

"Properly harnessed, this small sphere could transform not only Metro City, but life for those on the Surface as well," Dr. Elefun said, smiling hopefully.

Then he caught sight of President Stone and the soldiers in the balcony. His smile faded.

"Imagine cleaning up the earth's water," Dr. Elefun continued. "Imagine bringing back the forests, imagine overcoming the effects of centuries of pollution . . ."

Next to President Stone, Dr. Tenma watched his

friend in admiration.

"I know he's a bit of a dreamer, but he's a brilliant scientist," he assured the president.

"He's a dangerous idiot who happens to have a high IQ," President Stone snapped.

Onstage, a panel opened up on the floor and another pillar rose up. This one held a glowing red globe in a glass box.

"Unfortunately, there's no such thing as a free lunch," Dr. Elefun said. "When we extracted the positive blue energy from the fragment, we were left with this highly unstable byproduct. Red energy."

A larger hologram of the red ball of light was projected next to Dr. Elefun. While the blue energy looked peaceful, the red energy looked unstable and angry.

"I like that one," President Stone remarked. "Women voters are very partial to the color red, you know."

Down below, Dr. Elefun continued his presentation. "Until we discover how to safely dispose of it . . . "

Suddenly, soldiers stormed the stage. They grabbed Dr. Elefun and then picked up the cases holding the red and blue globes.

"What are you doing? Stop!" Dr. Elefun yelled. "Keep the cores apart or you'll kill us all!"

President Stone stepped onto the stage. "Do as he

says!" he warned his soldiers.

The soldiers stepped apart, keeping the cores separate.

Dr. Elefun's face was red with anger. "This is outrageous! Unprecedented! What are you intending to do with them?"

"Ha. I'm going to give the people of this city a reason to reelect me," President Stone said, smiling like a snake.

"How?" Dr. Elefun asked.

"The only way I can, Doctor. I'm gonna kick some butt!"

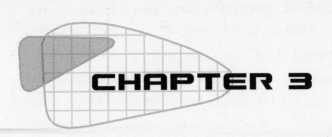

CHAPTER 3

Toby struggled to escape the soldier's grip, but his captor was too strong. The soldier stopped in front of a blank, white door. With one free hand, the soldier took a card key from his pocket and slid it into a card reader on the side of the door. The door slid open.

"This is so unfair!" Toby protested.

The soldier pushed Toby through the door into a small holding cell. It was bare except for a single white stool.

"Now cool off, hotshot," the soldier warned.

Toby took a look around the tiny room. He launched himself onto the soldier, pleading.

"Please don't leave me in here! I can't stand small places. Anywhere but here!" Toby begged.

The soldier plucked Toby off of his chest. "Gee, kid, you're like thirteen years old. It's time you grew a backbone."

He backed up, closing the door behind him.

Toby grinned. "And you're, like, twenty-two. It's time you grew a brain."

Toby held up the card key he had swiped from the soldier during his fake breakdown. He opened the door and peeked out. The soldier was goofing off down the hallway, trying to impress a girl. Perfect. Toby tiptoed down the corridor toward his father's lab.

Inside the lab, Dr. Elefun, President Stone, and the soldiers were gathered around Dr. Tenma. A female scientist sat behind a U-shaped control center. Beyond the control panel was a testing lab full of strange equipment. The Blue Core and Red Core had been placed in two stasis chambers, which were hovering on each side of the room.

o———o

"How could you be a party to this, Tenma?" Dr. Elefun asked in a hurt voice.

"Oh, come on, Elefun," Dr. Tenma replied. "You know as well as I do, without military funding, all of our research—including yours—would grind to a halt."

He called out to a female scientist sitting at a control panel.

"Start it up."

A panel behind the lab opened to reveal a cavernous testing area. A huge robot lowered down from the ceiling on wires. The terrifying robot looked like a gigantic war machine protected by heavy body armor. Its legs were as big as tanks, and its arms were just as massive. Its small head was tucked into a large upper body with wide shoulders like a linebacker. Two dead, expressionless eyes looked out of its face.

The wires released, and the Peacekeeper stood on its own.

"Load the Blue Core," Dr. Tenma ordered.

The female scientist operated a remote and the robot's chest opened like a sliding door. Lights blinked on inside.

As the scientist controlled it, the Peacekeeper turned and moved toward the waiting Blue Core.

"Hold on," President Stone said.

The scientist stopped, and the Peacekeeper froze in position.

The president turned to Dr. Tenma and Dr. Elefun. "This Blue Core . . . it's all sweetness and light, right? I mean, save the dolphins, give peace a chance?"

Dr. Elefun nodded. "It's pure positive energy."

"Call me a dreamer, but I think we'll get a bit

more bang for our buck using the red one," President Stone said cheerfully.

"Ha!" Dr. Elefun laughed. Then he saw President Stone looked completely serious. "Oh, you're not joking?"

"Sir, we're not putting something that dangerous into . . . something that dangerous," Dr. Tenma added.

"Listen, Tenma, I've got an election to win," President Stone snapped. "I need my robot to be a fighter, not a lover."

He nodded to the scientist at the controls. "Load the red one."

"I won't," she said firmly.

"Then I'll do it!" the president said. "Move over, sweetheart."

He roughly nudged the scientist out of her seat and grabbed the controls.

"No!" Dr. Elefun cried.

He and Dr. Tenma jumped forward, but the soldiers held them back.

President Stone worked the controls. The Peacekeeper awkwardly stomped over to the Red Core.

"Ha! It's like a stupid video game," the president laughed.

A claw emerged from within the robot's chest.

It grasped the Red Core and brought it inside the compartment.

"Core loaded," the Peacekeeper reported in a deep, mechanical voice.

"Piece of cake!" President Stone cheered.

General Heckler, a stocky man with a smooth bald head, motioned to the soldiers.

"Activate weapon drones," he ordered.

Small flying robot drones appeared, soaring into the testing area. They fired missile blasts at the Peacekeeper, but the mammoth robot easily deflected them, blasting them with laser weapons attached to its arms.

Toby slipped into the lab during this demonstration. His eyes widened at the sight of the Peacekeeper.

"Wow. I gotta get a better look," Toby whispered.

He snuck past the soldiers, moving closer and closer to the testing area. Another robot drone swooped down on the Peacekeeper, firing away. The Peacekeeper lunged forward and absorbed the drone into its shoulder. Once the drone became part of the Peacekeeper, it started firing away at the approaching drones.

"It's using that drone against the others," President Stone said, surprised. "How is that possible?"

"It's called adaptive technology," Dr. Tenma

explained. "It can absorb and control anything."

Toby still couldn't see well past the heads of the soldiers. He ducked under the control panel, unnoticed, and snuck into the testing area.

One after another, the drones were absorbed into the Peacekeeper's body. The already-huge robot grew in size and power each time. President Stone was delighted.

"I may have flunked out of college, but I was right about the Red Core," he bragged. "You scientists think you're the only ones with brains."

Zap!

With no more drones to attack, the Peacekeeper turned its attention to the humans in the room. A missile blast whizzed past the president's face, narrowly missing him.

"What the heck is it doing?" he asked in alarm.

The Peacekeeper's eyes flashed red as it stomped toward them. Thinking quickly, Dr. Tenma reached for the controls and hit the Emergency Shield Activation Panel. A glass shield dropped down just in time to protect them from the Peacekeeper's fire. The blasts buckled a part of the shield, but it didn't break.

Toby stood up and pounded on the glass. The shield had trapped him with the Peacekeeper!

"Dad! Help me! Dad! Dad!" he yelled.

"Toby!" Dr. Tenma cried.

Panicked, he tried to raise the shield. But the blast from the Peacekeeper had damaged it. It wouldn't move.

"Help me, Dad!" Toby pleaded.

The Peacekeeper was determined to break the shield. It raised its left arm and aimed a huge cannon-like weapon at the glass.

Boom!

A blinding flash of light filled the lab. The area behind the shield filled with smoke. When the smoke cleared, there was no sign of Toby.

"Toby!" Dr. Tenma cried.

The Peacekeeper held up a hand. Instead of blasting the shield again, it absorbed the shield into its body.

"Fire now!" President Stone ordered.

Soldiers fired at the Peacekeeper with their guns, but he simply absorbed the blasts.

Dr. Elefun thought quickly. He reached for one of the large power cables with Blue Core energy running through it. Then he bravely charged at the Peacekeeper, jamming it into the Red Core energy in his chest.

The Peacekeeper's power shorted out. The enormous robot fell back with a huge crash. The absorbed drones shot back out of its body.

Dr. Tenma frantically searched the lab.

"Where's Toby? Where's my son?"

Tenma picked up Toby's baseball hat. It was all that was left after the huge explosion. Tears welled in the scientist's eyes.

Dr. Elefun approached and put a hand on his shoulder. "I am so sorry, Tenma," he said gently.

President Stone had only one concern. He walked up to the fallen Peacekeeper.

"It was just the Red Core," he mused. "With the Blue Core, it would have worked perfectly, right?"

Dr. Tenma cradled Toby's hat. "Toby, it's all my fault," he said. His eyes took on a look of determination.

CHAPTER 4

Over the next few weeks, Dr. Tenma never left his lab. He worked day and night on his new robot—a robot that looked just like Toby.

Dr. Tenma had created every kind of robot there was. But this—this would be his masterpiece. He used whatever spare mechanical parts and weaponry he could find in his lab. He found a strand of Toby's hair inside the hat, and used that to upload Toby's memories into the robot. He didn't take a break—and he didn't let his assistants slow down, either.

He would not stop until he had Toby back.

Dr. Elefun arrived at the Ministry of Science one night, carrying a steel case. He headed up to the lab to find Tenma and his scientists busy at work. An older male scientist wearing glasses and a beret approached him.

"He hasn't eaten or slept in days," he told Dr. Elefun.

"I know," Dr. Elefun replied.

He lowered his voice. "He's gone crazy, hasn't he?"

"If your son dies like that, and you don't go crazy, you're not human," Dr. Elefun answered.

He moved on toward Dr. Tenma. The two scientists locked eyes.

"Clear the lab," Dr. Tenma ordered his assistants.

As the scientists quietly left, Dr. Elefun saw the robot skeleton on the lab table behind his friend. He gasped. The shape of the robot looked just like Toby.

Without a word, Dr. Tenma activated a machine next to the table. A laser net made up of criss-crossed strands of green laser light moved over the robot skeleton. As the net passed over the robot, it left behind a realistic layer of skin. Now the robot looked even more like Toby.

"It looks just like him, doesn't it?" Dr. Tenma asked. "A perfect replica. Plus, I've uploaded all of Toby's memories. It'll think it *is* Toby."

"Don't expect too much, Tenma," Dr. Elefun warned.

"It has the most advanced defense system ever created," Dr. Tenma said proudly. "I won't lose him again."

He paused. "Did you bring what I asked?"

"I couldn't refuse a grieving father," Dr. Elefun replied.

He placed the steel box on the table and opened it to reveal the Blue Core glowing inside. Then he gripped Dr. Tenma by the shoulders. His friend had such high hopes. He didn't want him to be disappointed. He had been through so much pain already.

"The core is . . . unpredictable," Dr. Elefun told him. "I can't guarantee what effect . . . "

Dr. Tenma was not about to give up. "It's going to make it perfect—perfect! Just like Toby was."

He took the core and faced the robot boy. Dr. Tenma placed the Blue Core in an opening in the robot's chest.

Nothing happened for a moment. Then . . .

Cables lowered from the ceiling and attached themselves to the robot's head and back. Then the cables began to retract, lifting the robot with them. Bursts of energy shot from the robot's core chest.

Bam!

A huge explosion rocked the lab. The table collapsed underneath the boy. He rolled onto the floor, landing flat on his back.

The room quieted down. The two scientists stared, unable to move.

The robot's eyes opened. They looked blank and lifeless. He turned to look at the two men. He stared blankly at them for a moment as the complicated program whirred to life inside his robot brain.

Suddenly, his face lit up with a smile. He looked as human as any real boy.

"Dad?" the robot asked.

"Toby," Dr. Tenma said, breathless.

The robot stood up and took a few unsteady steps. Then he leaped into Dr. Tenma's arms.

"Dad!"

Dr. Tenma wrapped the robot boy in a blanket.

"Welcome back, son," he said tearfully. "Thank you, Elefun. I'm going to take it . . . *him* home now. Quality time. Bonding. All the good things."

Dr. Elefun gazed curiously at the new Toby, as Tenma carried him to the door.

"Bye, Dr. Elefun," the robot said cheerfully.

Dr. Elefun was startled—the robot even sounded like Toby. "Uh . . . bye . . . Toby."

He watched them exit the lab, shaking his head.

"Incredible," he muttered.

Poor Toby Tenma was gone forever. But thanks to his father, he would live on in robot form.

Astro Boy was born!

CHAPTER 5

Astro didn't know he was a robot. He just thought he was Toby Tenma, Dr. Tenma's son. That night, he drifted into a peaceful sleep.

When he opened his eyes again, sunlight was streaming through his bedroom window. His dad sat at the edge of his bed, clutching his baseball cap.

"Dad?" Astro asked sleepily.

"Good morning, son," Dr. Tenma said. "How do you feel?"

"Uh, kind of weird," Astro admitted. "Have I been sick or something?"

"No, you're fine, Toby," Dr. Tenma said. "You're perfect, you're wonderful."

Astro was relieved. "That's good, cause . . ."

Dr. Tenma interrupted him by gripping him in a strong hug. Astro was surprised. His dad wasn't exactly big on hugs.

"Are you okay?" Astro asked.

"Come downstairs for breakfast," his father said, smiling gently.

Dr. Tenma went downstairs, where Orrin was frantically scurrying around the kitchen. He took his seat as Orrin slapped bowls and plates in front of him.

"Breakfast is served, sir," he said. "Whole grain cereal, prune juice, figs . . . "

"Ah! It's past eight o'clock!" Astro yelled from his room upstairs.

Orrin went into panic mode. Master Toby could be very unpleasant when his breakfast was late. He rolled off to get the rest of the food.

Astro ran through the kitchen doorway.

"You should have woken me earlier, Dad. I'm going to be late for school," he said, worried.

Bam! Orrin bumped into Astro, carrying a tray of croissants. The pastries spilled all over the floor. Orrin bent down to pick them up.

Astro reached down to help him.

"Orrin, are you okay? Your battery levels look a little low this morning," Astro said with concern.

Orrin spun his head around to look at Astro, surprised. Master Toby had never asked about his health before.

"Orrin?" Astro asked.

"Thank you for asking, Master Toby," Orrin said. "I'm fine, you know. Mustn't grumble."

"Sit down, Toby," Dr. Tenma said. "I want to talk to you."

"Sure, Dad," Astro said cheerfully. He took a seat at the table.

"It's about school," Dr. Tenma began. "I've decided you shouldn't go anymore, son. I'm going to teach you at home myself."

"Sounds good to me," Astro said. "Hey, Orrin. Looks like we're going to be hanging out together."

Orrin nearly dropped the teapot he was carrying. Master Toby wasn't acting like himself at all. Dr. Tenma would not like that one bit.

"Together? Oh, well, that'll be very nice . . . Master Toby . . . oh dear."

Orrin dropped the teapot after all. It fell on the table with a clatter.

"Would you please stop talking to the robot?" Dr. Tenma asked Astro, annoyed. "They're not like you and me."

"Sorry," Astro said. "Hey, if you're going to be home-schooling me, what about the Ministry, your job?"

"My job now is to be your father," Dr. Tenma replied.

Still nervous, Orrin walked into a wall.

"Ouch!"

———

Astro's lessons began right away. Dr. Tenma and Astro set themselves up in Astro's bedroom. Astro sat at his holo-desk. Dr. Tenma hit a switch, and one whole wall of the room turned into a giant, glowing computer screen.

"Let's start you out with something familiar," Dr. Tenma suggested.

The screen began to fill with line after line of mathematical calculations. Astro gave his father a puzzled look.

"Four-dimensional calculus. It's your favorite," Dr. Tenma said eagerly.

The memory of calculus started to form in Astro's brain. "I *guess* it is," he said. He sat there, staring at the screen. It didn't look like fun at all.

Orrin poked his head in the room. "If sir wishes, uh, perhaps I could help Master Toby with—"

Dr. Tenma shot him an annoyed look.

"I'll just get on and do the . . . dusting," Orrin said quickly. Then he rolled away.

Astro nodded to his father. "Okay . . . watch."

Astro quickly touched the screen, and the numbers

and symbols began to move around. Dr. Tenma watched, pleased. Astro solved every problem correctly.

"Bravo, wonderful, excellent, Toby!" he praised. "First rate, son, first rate."

"You ain't seen nothing yet," Astro replied, grinning. He tapped a few more keys.

The symbols on the screen became three-dimensional, twisting and floating. The numbers and figures turned into an animated cowboy riding on a horse. The cowboy swung his lasso and yodeled an old cowboy song. Astro laughed with delight.

Dr. Tenma frowned and switched off the computer screen.

"Let's get back to basics."

Dr. Tenma led Astro to his library, which was filled with rows and rows of books kept in glass-fronted bookcases. He unlocked one and took out an armful of thick, dusty volumes. He plunked the books on Astro's desk.

"Remember this one?" he asked, tapping the top book. "Kant's *Critique of Pure Reason*. I used to read it to you in bed when you were little."

Astro coughed from the dust. "To put me to sleep?"

"Yes!" Dr. Tenma said. "You asked for it every night."

Astro frowned. "That's not quite what I—"

"Just try rereading these," his father suggested. "Get the old brain humming again. *Whirrrrr!*"

He gave Astro a thumbs-up and then left him alone in the library. Astro stared at the pile of books. He opened one to see more pages of mathematic equations.

"Hmm . . . next," Astro said. He might have liked this stuff once, but for some reason he wanted something a little more . . . fun.

Astro didn't realize it, but the Blue Core had infused him with positive energy. Toby had never taken the time to really enjoy life, or even to care about others. But thanks to the Blue Core, Astro was different.

The next book he opened showed pages of Leonardo da Vinci's drawings. Now this was more like it. The great artist and inventor had sketched plans for all kinds of flying machines years before the first airplane took flight. Astro's brain did start humming—but not in the way his father wanted.

A few hours later, the library was filled with paper flying machines Astro had created using the pages from the book. With Orrin's help, he had recreated them all—and they worked! Some looked like strange birds; others looked like helicopters with spinning propellers. Astro watched, smiling, as Orrin happily chased them around the room.

"Ah, beautiful, I got it! I got it!" the robot cried, reaching for one. He just missed catching it. "So close!"

"Way to go, Orrin. You're the man!" Astro cheered. He put his baseball cap on Orrin's head.

If Orrin weren't made of metal, he would have blushed. "Yes, I am . . . I am the man," he said awkwardly.

Astro had stacked a bunch of books on the desk to create the perfect launching point. He climbed on top of them.

"Check this out."

He let a complex paper airplane fly. It joined the other aircrafts, gracefully swooping and diving between them.

"I'm impressed," Orrin said. "Not knocked out, but impressed."

"That's nothing. Watch this!" Astro said.

The plane divided into three smaller planes. They zipped around the library.

"Oh, now that is impressive, Master Toby!" he praised.

"Just Toby is fine, Orrin," Astro said.

The little planes quickly spun out of control. One of them knocked over a glass vase. The other slammed into a picture on the wall, bumping it off the nail.

Dr. Tenma stepped into the library. "Toby—"

Whack! One of the paper planes hit him in the side of the head.

"What are you doing?" Dr. Tenma asked. "I told you to read these books, not destroy them."

"I . . . I just wanted to test Da Vinci's theories," Astro explained.

"I perhaps encouraged Master Toby, sir," Orrin said, coming to Astro's defense.

Dr. Tenma noticed the hat on Orrin's head.

"You should not be wearing that hat," he snapped. "A robot should not be wearing my son's . . . Toby's hat."

Orrin took off the hat and gave it to Dr. Tenma. He rolled out of the library, sadly hanging his head.

"Dad, it's fine," Astro said. "I don't even like that hat."

"I think you should go to your room," Dr. Tenma said sternly.

"But, Dad—" Astro protested.

"Do as you're told."

Astro left the room, dejected. Dr. Tenma paced back and forth, gripping Toby's hat in his hands. He pressed a button on a device on the desk. A second later, a holograph of Dr. Elefun appeared in the room.

"Tenma? What's wrong?" Dr. Elefun asked.

"I think I've made a terrible mistake," Dr. Tenma said. "I thought he would be like Toby, but he's not. He's . . . strange. He's very strange."

"Strange how?" his friend asked.

"He's brilliant, as Toby was, but different." Dr. Tenma paused. "He makes jokes. I don't like it."

"Jokes? Oh dear," Dr. Elefun replied. "Well, you can't expect him to be a carbon copy. Give him time, Tenma."

"You don't understand!" Dr. Tenma said. "He was meant to replace Toby, but every time I look at him, it just reminds me that Toby's gone and he's never coming back."

Dr. Elefun didn't like the tone of his friend's voice. "Don't do anything rash," he advised. "I'm coming over. Maybe I can make some kind of adjustments to him."

Under his breath, he added, "Or to you."

CHAPTER 6

Dr. Tenma lived on the top floor of one of the tallest skyscrapers in Metro City. The glass windows always sparkled in the sunlight. They were never streaked or dirty—thanks to robots, of course.

From a distance, the window-cleaning robots looked like flying birds. Up close, you could see they worked in teams. A robot that looked like a spray bottle would squirt window cleaner on the glass. Another robot equipped with a squeegee and a helicopter propeller wiped the glass clean.

A flock of robots were at work on Dr. Tenma's windows when Astro was sent to his room. He flopped on his bed, sad. There was a photo on his night table of Toby and his dad. Toby was holding an astrophysics trophy, grinning. Dr. Tenma looked very proud.

"What's different?" Astro wondered. "I haven't

seen Dad angry before."

He sighed, quiet for a moment. Then he heard an electronic squawking behind him. He turned to see two robots outside, cleaning his window. They chattered away in the electronic babble that robots used to talk to one another.

"Check out the haircut on that one," said the spray bottle, Mr. Squirt. "It looks like he's got horns."

"Ha-ha! Horns! Good one!" laughed Mr. Squeegee, his partner.

"What do you mean, horns? It's gel!" Astro protested.

Astro gasped.

"Wait! I can understand you!" he cried. But that should have been impossible. Humans couldn't understand robot language.

"Whoa, that's creepy," said Mr. Squeegee.

"What is?" asked Mr. Squirt.

"It's like he can understand us," Mr. Squeegee replied.

"Don't be stupid!" said Mr. Squirt.

"I can hear what you're saying!" Astro told them.

Mr. Squeegee squirted the window with liquid. "It's almost like he can hear what we're saying," he said, ignoring Astro.

"There's no way. He's a human," said Mr. Squirt. "Come on. Let's go leak oil on some statues."

"Ha-ha!" laughed Mr. Squeegee. "Okay."

He moved to wipe off the liquid on the glass when he screamed in fright. Astro had opened the window and was staring right at them.

"How can I understand what you're saying?" he asked. "You're robots!"

The two robots nervously backed up. "We don't want any trouble," said Mr. Squirt.

Astro grabbed him before he could fly off. "Wait up. I just want to know what's going on. What's happened to me?"

Mr. Squirt struggled to get away. "Hey, hey, calm down," Astro said. "I'm not gonna hurt you. You're safe, little fella."

Astro glanced down and gasped. He was hanging out of the window, hundreds of stories above the ground.

"Okay, guys, let's back up very carefully," he said calmly.

But Mr. Squirt just wanted to get away. He sprayed Astro in the eyes.

"Aaaaaaaaaaargh!" Astro screamed.

He tumbled out of the window, plummeting to the ground.

"Oh, that's tragic, that is," said Mr. Squirt.

"Yeah," said Mr. Squeegee. "You still want to go leak oil on some statues?"

"Heck to the yeah!" agreed Mr. Squirt. "Come on, baby!"

The two robots flew away. Astro closed his eyes as the pavement rushed up to meet him. In a matter of seconds, it would all be over . . .

Then something strange happened. Astro's body flipped into an upright position, with his feet facing the ground. Jets fired from the soles of his shoes. He hovered safely, inches above the ground.

Astro opened his eyes, not sure if he was dreaming. He wasn't. This was really happening.

Curious, Astro tried pushing up. He shot up quickly, losing his balance. But he was still hovering in the air. Astro tried again.

Slam! He hit the wall of the building, but he wasn't hurt. Laughing, he raised his arms above his head and took off into the sky.

Astro zipped past Mr. Squirt and Mr. Squeegee. The two robots squirted on themselves in shock.

Astro waved at the robots, but the motion sent him rocketing downward. An expressway tunnel loomed ahead, and Astro wasn't sure how to steer around it. He covered his eyes, hoping not to hit anything.

He zipped straight into the tunnel. Opening his eyes, he found he could weave in and out of the cars and trucks. He was getting the hang of it.

Astro emerged from the tunnel and soared up into the clouds. He had never felt so free.

He could fly!

Astro practiced diving in and out of the clouds. It was beautiful up here in the blue sky, with Metro City glimmering below. The more he flew, the bolder he got. Soon he was doing flips and cartwheels from cloud to cloud.

Astro flew as high as he could, then dove down through the clouds, heading back home. Now he was going so fast, he couldn't stop himself. Once again, he found himself plummeting toward the ground. Astro tried to turn upright again, but he couldn't do it.

Astro braced himself for the impact. Once again, something amazing happened. He dove right through the dirt, almost like he was swimming through water. He tunneled through the ground and exploded up from the top of a snow-covered mountain.

"This is so cool!" Astro cried, as he hovered over Metro City. "I gotta show Dad."

CHAPTER 7

President Stone paced the floor of his Command Center. Radar screens on the walls reported on the traffic in the air space above and around Metro City. Video monitors helped him keep an eye on the comings and goings of his residents.

General Heckler sat at a control desk, headphones on his ears. The president's advisors sat in metal chairs, cowering as their chief ranted and raved.

"How can my approval ratings be this low?" he fumed. "I was very popular in high school. I've cut taxes for a lot of very influential friends. What more do people want?"

General Heckler interrupted him. "We're tracking an unidentified object flying over Metro City, sir."

President Stone studied the radar screen. A flying dot moved across the city. "The Surface dwellers are firing at *us*? This is what I've been waiting for! Declare war on them! This is going to get me reelected!"

A soldier marched up to him. "This didn't come from the Surface, sir," he reported.

"It's my opponent," Stone guessed. "He's taken the gloves off. He's playing hardball."

The flying dot turned bright blue.

"It's Blue Core energy, sir!" the soldier cried.

President Stone's face darkened. "What? Elefun told me the Blue Core was destroyed. Get me a location and mobilize all units. I want that thing now!"

Astro had no idea he had been detected by the radar. He flew back home and landed on the balcony of his father's study. Orrin and Dr. Elefun were talking to Dr. Tenma. Their voices carried through the open sliding doors.

"Where is he? Where's Toby?" Dr. Elefun asked.

"I sent him to his room," Dr. Tenma said. "Please, just deactivate him and take him away. I can't bear to see his face again."

Astro gasped. Could they be talking about him?

"Come on, Tenma," Dr. Elefun pleaded. "You can't just throw him away like a piece of junk."

"Dad? What's going on?" Astro asked.

The two men turned and stared at Astro.

"Why are you talking about me like this?" he asked.

Dr. Elefun paused. "Toby, there's been a bit of a misunderstanding. You're not entirely an ordinary boy."

"I know," Astro said. He looked at Dr. Tenma. "Dad, I can fly! I can drill my way through solid rock. It's amazing."

Dr. Tenma turned his back on Astro. "How could I think this would work?"

"What's wrong with me? Why don't you love me anymore?" Astro asked.

Dr. Elefun faced his friend. "He's programmed with the memories of your own son, Tenma."

"Programmed?" Astro asked.

"Doesn't that mean anything to you?" asked Dr. Elefun.

"He's not my son," Dr. Tenma said coldly. "He's a robot who *looks* like my son."

Astro couldn't believe it. "Dad," he pleaded.

"I'm not your dad. You're not Toby. You're a copy of Toby," Dr. Tenma said. "A failed experiment, a robot, not my son. You're a robot, and I don't want you anymore!"

"No! No!" Astro wailed.

He turned back to the balcony.

"Toby! Wait!" Dr. Elefun yelled. He grabbed Astro

and looked into his eyes. "I can't see into the future, but I'm sure there's a place for you. You just have to find it."

"He was my father. This was my home. It's all I know," Astro said sadly.

"Everyone has their destiny, Toby," Dr. Elefun said.

"Didn't you hear him? I'm not Toby," Astro replied.

He rocketed off the balcony, taking one last look at his home. Orrin rolled onto the balcony, gazing sadly at Astro.

Astro flew off into the setting sun. He settled on the highest building he could find and sat there, thinking.

He stared hard at his hands. He looked human. He *felt* human. Could he really be a robot?

Blue light shot from Astro's eyes, acting like an X-ray. Underneath his skin he could see a network of wires and circuits.

"It's true," he murmured.

Suddenly, blinding lights hit Astro's eyes. He shielded himself from the glare. Two military planes were circling him.

One of the pilots radioed President Stone's Command Center.

"Sir, we located the signal's source, but it's . . . a kid. Readings for the Core are off the chart!"

"Is that Tenma's boy?" General Heckler asked.

"Of course not!" President Stone fumed behind him. "Tenma must have lost his mind. Bring it in."

The pilot radioed the other plane. "This is Stinger One. Set weapons for capture."

The two planes approached Astro.

"Oh no," Astro said. In a shot, he rocketed off into the night.

"Whoa! The subject just took off!" the pilot exclaimed.

"Commander, engage the subject with intent to capture," President Stone ordered.

The planes took off after Astro. Green tentacles lined with suction cups shot out from the planes, trying to grab him. Astro dodged each one.

"What do you guys want?" he called back.

"Command Center. We have it in our sights!" the pilot reported.

Astro dove down into Metro City to avoid the planes. They couldn't fly low, but they sent their tentacles after him.

One tentacle grabbed a dog by mistake. Another pulled a tablecloth off a table in a restaurant, leaving the dishes on top intact. The diners gasped in surprise.

Astro flew over the park. A man was kneeling on one knee, about to propose marriage to his girlfriend.

She sat on a park bench.

Whoosh! A tentacle grabbed her, too.

The pilot of the second plane radioed the Command Center. "This is Stinger Two. I'm ah . . . gonna take all these things back."

"Get him!" President Stone shouted.

Astro zipped around a building, disappearing from view. The pilot of Stinger One hovered in the air, confused.

"Where'd he go?"

Astro flew underneath both planes, bending their weapons so they couldn't fire. Then he flew up and slammed into Stinger One's windshield.

"Eee-yaaah!" the pilot cried. He pressed every button on his controls, but all it did was turn on his windshield wipers. Astro grinned.

Then he felt a tentacle wrap around his waist. He looked down to see the tentacles from both planes wrapped around him.

"Oh no," Astro said.

"We've got him! We're coming home!" said the Stinger One pilot.

Astro struggled to get free of the tentacles. Then his eyes lit up. He had remembered something.

His rockets were in the bottoms of his feet.

He could fly *up*.

"Haaaahhhhh!" Astro yelled.

He shot straight up in the air, pulling both aircraft below him. The pilots screamed.

Then Astro dove down between two skyscrapers, dragging the planes behind him. They slammed into the buildings. Astro flew forward now, pulling with all his might.

"Arrrrrrrrrrrrrrrrgh!"

Astro pulled free from the tentacles. The force tore Stinger One in half. The pilot screamed as he fell through the sky.

"Oh no!" Astro cried. He didn't want anyone to get hurt. He zoomed to the soldier and caught him in midair.

Back in the Command Center, President Stone was furious.

"Send in the Spirit of Freedom," he ordered.

His advisors gasped in shock.

"The Spirit of Freedom? That weapon doesn't officially exist, sir!"

"I'm trying to win an election, not run a sewing circle," Stone snapped. "Destroy the robot, then collect the core."

Astro dropped the soldier safely on top of a building.

"You're safe," he told him.

But a swarm of Stinger planes hovered in the air above him, their weapons extended.

"Again? What's with you guys?" Astro asked.

The rescued pilot gave Astro a quick hug. "I love you!" he said.

Astro flew off to face the Stingers. "Come on, then!" he challenged.

Then a dark shadow loomed over them all. A huge gunship floated above them. The Stingers flew away like frightened birds. The pilot jumped off of the building in terror.

"Fire!" President Stone commanded.

Bam! Bam! Bam! The Spirit of Freedom assaulted the rooftop with a missile blast. The force of the explosion knocked Astro down. He tried to pull himself up, but he was hurt.

President Stone grinned. "Finish it."

Bam! Bam! Bam! The missiles headed straight for Astro.

President Stone high-fived General Heckler. Then they chest-butted, and Heckler toppled over. Stone kicked him for luck.

Astro couldn't dodge all of the missiles. They slammed into him, sending him sailing off of the rooftop.

President Stone glanced at the monitor and frowned. The blue dot was falling to the bottom of the screen. How could that be?

"Hey, where is it going?" President Stone yelled. "Come back! Come back! I am declaring a state of emergency! Leave for all military personnel is canceled until Tenma's boy is found."

CHAPTER 8

Astro wasn't sure exactly what happened after the missiles hit. He just remembered falling . . . and falling . . . and falling. Then everything went black.

He opened his eyes and found himself face-to-face with a burned-out robot head.

"Aaaaargh!" he yelled.

But the robot head was still alive. "Welcome to your new home, kid," he said cheerfully.

"Aaaaaaaah!"

Startled, Astro fell back and landed on a robot with one arm.

"Hello," the robot greeted him.

"Aaaaaaaah!" he screamed again.

He stood up and backed away. Looking down, he realized he was standing on top of a huge mountain of discarded robots.

This is where the old robots from Metro City end up, he realized.

All around him, robots began to rise up like zombies from the grave. They walked toward Astro, excited.

"New batteries! He's got new batteries!" cried one jealous robot.

A tiny robot approached him with his hands out. "Spare a few volts for a fellow Sparky?" he asked.

The first robot sadly shook his head. "New batteries . . ."

Most of the robots were not functioning properly. A French waiter robot walked up to a robot on fire.

"Table for one. Smoking or non-smoking?" the waiter asked.

"Smoking! I'm definitely smoking!" the burning robot answered frantically.

The robots began to surround Astro.

"You're one of us now," said the robot head. "Happy to meet you."

"Oh no," Astro protested. "I'm not one of you guys."

"You're a robot, ain't you?" the robot head asked.

"Er . . . yes, but . . . "

"Well, welcome to the scrap heap!" the head said. "This is where we all end up sooner or later."

Astro shook his head. "No way. I'm not ready yet."

The robots began to chant. "One of us. One of us. One of us."

They circled him, getting closer and closer. Some reached out to grab him with their metal hands.

"Hey, get off of me! What are you doing?" Astro yelled.

The robot head suddenly looked up.

"Incoming!"

Astro gazed up to see another load of discarded robots crashing down from Metro City. The impact sent him tumbling down the mountain. He got to his feet and looked around.

The robots down here had all lost power a long time ago. He breathed a sigh of relief. It was quiet down here, at least.

Still, there was nothing but mounds and mounds of dead robots as far as he could see.

"What do I do?" Astro wondered.

He slumped down on a pile of spare parts and put his head in his hands.

"Dad ... "

Then Astro heard something rustling in the next trash pile. Had those weird robots come after him?

"Who's there?" he called out.

The sound stopped. Astro's eyes began to glow, lighting up the darkness. They settled on a pair of glowing eyes staring right back at him.

Astro tensed, expecting some kind of attack. Instead, a robot dog bounded out of the trash pile. The dog looked like it had been made out of a metal garbage can with a dome-shaped lid. Blue eyes glowed in its face along with a round, metal nose.

It ran up to Astro with its tail wagging and then fell back, exposing its belly.

"Woof. Woof."

"Whoa," Astro said, scooting back. He wasn't sure if he could trust any of the robots down here.

The dog crawled into Astro's lap and began to lick his face with a metal tongue. Astro couldn't help smiling.

"You like me, huh?" He checked the tag around the dog's neck. "Trashcan. So are you lost, Trashcan?" Astro sighed. "I know I sure am."

The dog jumped from Astro's lap and started pulling on his sleeve.

"What is it, boy?" Astro asked.

Trashcan wagged his tail.

"You want me to come with you?" Astro asked.

He wagged his tail again.

"Someone's in trouble?"

Trashcan bounded off. Astro raced after him. The dog weaved through the narrow valleys between the scrap heaps. Finally, he skidded to a stop. Astro stepped behind him.

The dog had stopped in front of a hole in the ground. Astro peered into the darkness. The hole looked really, really deep.

"Is this it?" he asked Trashcan. "Hello!"

His voice echoed back at him.

"This could be miles down," Astro said. "This hole looks pretty—"

Bam! Trashcan bounded into Astro's chest, pushing him down the hole.

"Deeeeeeeeeeeeeeeeeeep!" Astro wailed.

Astro felt himself falling and falling once more. He was about to activate his jets when he came to a sudden stop.

Stunned, he tried to regain his bearings. He seemed to be caught in a net. He looked up and saw that the net was suspended from a tall crane.

The crane pulled him out of the hole and dumped him on the ground. Four grimy-looking kids ran up to him.

"Quick! Get the restraints on it. Hurry!" urged the oldest girl. She looked like she was about seventeen.

Her spiky, black hair was streaked with purple. Her jeans were patched, and she wore a tank top over a T-shirt over a long-sleeved shirt. She had bright red sneakers on her feet.

Two young kids responded to her order and tried to untangle the net. The girl and boy looked like twins. Both had curly, brown hair. The little girl wore hers in two puffy ponytails on top of her head.

A teenage boy with shaggy, brown hair patted Trashcan on the back. "Good work, boy. Treat for ya!"

He tossed Trashcan a wrench, and the dog happily chewed on it like it was a bone.

The twins kept trying to get hold of Astro.

"Knock it off!" he warned.

All four kids jumped back and stared at him.

"That's not a robot," said the older girl.

"It's a kid," said the little boy.

Astro stared back at them. Should he tell them the truth?

"Uh, that's right," he said. "I'm . . . I'm a kid like you."

The teenage boy tried to wrestle his wrench back from Trashcan. "Hey, give it back, you stupid garbage eater."

The oldest girl eyed Astro. She looked amused. "So where are you from, non-robot?"

"I'm from Metro City," Astro replied.

The girl began to gush with fake excitement, like a starstruck teen. "Metro City?" She turned to her friends. "Can you believe it? He's actually *talking* to me."

"Are you feeling okay?" asked a bewildered Astro.

"Omigosh, he talked to me twice!" the girl gushed. "This is definitely going in my diary as the most exciting day of my life!"

"Okay, I get it," Astro said. "You don't like people from Metro City."

The older boy got a dreamy look in his eyes. "Metro City. Robots waiting on you hand and foot. I'd love to visit, just for one day."

"They wouldn't let you in," the girl said harshly. "They have a strict 'No Losers from the Surface Allowed' policy. Anyway, why would you want to go someplace where people think you're garbage?"

Astro looked sad, remembering his dad.

The girl pulled a glowing cell phone from the rubble. "I mean, look at this! Can you believe someone just threw this away?"

The boy tried to touch it, but she whisked it from him. "Nu-uh! Finders keepers!"

She moved on, collecting bits and pieces of things and stuffing them into a sack.

"So what are you doing down here?" asked the boy.

"I don't know yet," Astro said. "Looking for something I guess . . . somewhere."

"Did you run away?" the youngest boy asked.

"Not exactly," Astro answered carefully. "They sort of suggested I find a new place . . . whatever that means."

The little girl shook her head. "Dude, it means they kicked you out."

The older girl called back to them. "Come on! Get with the program. We've got work to do."

The three kids started filling their own sacks with scraps. Astro trailed after them.

"Hey, maybe I could come with you guys?" he asked.

"Sorry, we don't need any more newbies," the older girl said.

Whoot! Whoot! Whoot!

The sound of a siren roared through the scrap yard. The ground began to rumble, and Astro could hear the sound of a rumbling engine.

"This has got to be an earthquake," he guessed.

"Nope! Wrong answer, Contestant Number Two!" the girl cried. She broke into a run. The others followed. Astro hesitated.

The girl looked behind her and saw that Astro wasn't moving. "Ugh! Come on!" she said urgently.

CHAPTER 9

The girl sounded serious. Astro looked behind them—there was nothing. But he ran anyway.

"What are we running from?" he shouted up ahead.

"The Scorpion Brothers!" the twins wailed.

Dirt began flying behind them. The ground broke open, and two terrifying metal claws emerged. Each claw grabbed one of the twins, dragging them out of sight.

"Widget! Sludge!" yelled the older girl. She looked behind her. "Oh no! The new kid's roadkill!"

Astro wanted to keep his secret from the kids—but he couldn't stand by while the twins were in danger. He tunneled through the ground until he reached them.

Bam! Bam! He pummeled the claws with two powerful punches. They released the twins. Astro grabbed one kid in each arm and flew back through the tunnel he had made.

When he reached the Surface, he set the twins down. They were completely dazed. Astro sat down beside them.

"What happened?' asked the little girl.

"I have no clue," Astro lied. "At least we're safe."

The twins suddenly looked terrified.

"Aaaaaargh!" they screamed.

"It's okay," Astro assured them. "There's nothing to worry about."

Two metal claws grabbed Astro from behind. Each claw was held by a scruffy-looking man dressed like a junkyard pirate. They carried Astro behind a scrap mound, away from Sludge and Widget.

"Looks like we got us a real live robot, Testo!" said one of the Scorpion Brothers.

"Whaddya mean 'we,' Ronnie? It's mine!" Testo argued. He pulled Astro toward him.

"Finders keepers!" Ronnie whined.

"Your momma!" Testo shot back.

"She's your momma, too!" Ronnie pointed out.

Astro had heard enough. "That's it. You're both grounded."

Astro grabbed the end of each claw and powered up his jets, flying into the air. He swung the claws around and around. With all his might, he hurled the two brothers into a trash heap far across the scrap yard.

Astro flew back to the ground and walked back to Widget and Sludge. He found the other two kids fussing over them.

"You're okay!" the older girl said, relieved.

"They got the new kid!" Widget said sadly.

Astro walked into view. He pretended to be out of breath.

"No, they didn't," he said.

Widget and Sludge cheered. They ran up to Astro and gave him a big hug.

"So what happened to the Scorpion Brothers?" the older girl asked.

Astro pointed behind him. The two Scorpion Brothers were dangling from the top of a trash heap, hanging by their claws.

Astro shrugged. "I just turned off their magnets."

"Magnets?" She sounded like she didn't believe him.

The teenage boy held out his hand. "I'm Zane."

"I'm Widget," said the little girl.

"I'm Sludge," said her brother. "I'm older than her."

"By ninety seconds," Widget quickly added.

"I'm Cora," said the oldest girl. "What's your name?"

"Er, it's . . . " Astro wasn't sure what to answer. Toby was part of him, but Toby *wasn't* him. He was somebody else. Somebody new.

Before Astro could reply, three robots appeared, whisking him away.

The robots' cry echoed behind them. "Viva la Roboto-lution!"

Cora shook her head. "What just happened?"

CHAPTER 10

The three robots that carried off Astro were not exactly a scary-looking bunch. One was tall and thin, with skinny arms and legs. The other had a big, bulky body with a television set on his chest. The third was a walking mini refrigerator.

"Did you see the human's faces?" asked the skinny one, in a British accent. "They were quaking in their capitalist boots!"

Astro gave his jets a quick blast, freeing himself. He landed in front of the three robots.

"Okay. What's this about?" he asked.

"Don't worry, brother. You're safe," assured the skinny bot.

The big bot spoke in a Russian accent. "You have been rescued by . . . "

All three saluted.

"THE ROBOT REVOLUTIONARY FRONT!" they shouted together.

"I'm Sparx, the brains," said the skinny one.

"And I'm Robotsky, the muscle," said the big one.

"And I'm Mike the Fridge," said the third robot. "I'm the fridge."

Astro looked around. He appeared to be in some kind of clubhouse hidden among the scrap heaps.

"You are now liberated!" Robotsky said. "Go ahead, comrade. Take your first step as a free robot."

Astro took a step forward—into a puddle of oil.

"Feels different, doesn't it?" Sparx asked.

"It feels wetter," Astro replied.

Sparx eyed Astro up and down. "You look like a pretty advanced model if I might say so, brother." He leaned in close, whispering, "Are you exempt from the laws of robotics?"

"Remind me?" Astro asked.

"A robot cannot harm a human, be the cause of any harm to a human, blah, blah, blah, boring, boring, boring," Robotsky recited.

"Well, I don't really want to harm anybody," Astro replied.

Sparky frowned. "Lugnuts! The RRF is dedicated to freeing robot-kind from human slavery by *any* means necessary."

"And he means any means necessary," added Mike the Fridge, sounding tough.

"Ruthless, we are," Sparx said, nodding.

"Show him, comrade!" Robotsky urged.

Sparx rifled through the messy hideout and produced a thick file of papers.

"Dozens of angry letters to the editors of major newspapers," Sparx said proudly. "We dared them to print them and they all refused. That's how scared of us they are."

"Wow," Astro said. That didn't sound too impressive to him, but he didn't want to hurt their feelings.

"'A revolution is impossible without a revolutionary situation,'" Sparx quoted.

"Is that Lenin?" Robotsky asked.

"I thought it was McCartney," Sparx replied.

Robotsky shook his barrel-shaped head. "No. McCartney's the 'Give War a Chance' guy."

Astro had no idea what these robots were talking about. The night was getting stranger and stranger.

"Well, I guess I'll be going," he said casually.

"What is your name, comrade?" Sparx asked.

"Er, Toby," Astro replied. He still thought of himself as Toby. Dr. Tenma's human son.

"That's not much of a name," Sparx said. "You want something with a bit more oomph to it."

"Something like the Ice-Maker," suggested Mike the Fridge.

"Or the Annihilator," said Sparx.

"Or Doris," offered Robotsky.

"Well, I guess I really will be going now," Astro said, slowly backing away.

As he spoke, Robotsky shut off his power. Then he powered back up.

"What about Astro?" he said.

Astro kind of liked the sound of that, but Sparx was annoyed. "Oh, be quiet. If you can't come up with a sensible suggestion then kindly mind your own business."

Robotsky looked at the floor. "Sorry."

"Think, think," Sparx muttered. "Wait. I got it! ASTRO!"

"Oh, that's marvelous, it is," gushed Robotsky.

"It's modern, a little space age—I love it!" Sparx decided.

Astro took another step back. "Okay, but I really gotta—"

"Tell Astro the plan!" Sparx said quickly.

The other two robots gasped.

"Tell him!" Sparx ordered.

"As you wish, comrade," Robotsky said.

The TV screen on his chest sparked to life. The face of a chubby man with a dark mustache appeared.

"This is Hamegg, owner of the World Wide Robot Games in town," Sparx said.

"We will now spit on his name," said Robotsky.

All three robots spit on the floor at the mention of his name.

Astro grimaced. "Nice."

"The robot games enslave our kind," Sparx explained. "We need to make an example of Hamegg. We want to do something so horrible . . . so frightening . . . so shocking that the humans will be forced to free all robots."

Astro was starting to feel nervous. Maybe these guys were more dangerous than they looked.

"What are you going to do?" he asked.

"The next robot games are in a week," Robotsky began.

"We're going to sneak into town in cunning disguises," Sparx continued.

Mike the Fridge joined in. "We're going to lie in wait for Hamegg . . . "

Astro waited for the payoff. "And?"

"And when he shows up . . . " Robotsky hesitated.

"Yes?" Astro asked impatiently.

"Now bear in mind that we're forced to follow the laws of robotics," Sparx reminded him.

"Okay," Astro said.

Sparx raised a fist in the air. "We're going to tickle him with a feather!"

"Viva la Roboto-lution!" the three robots yelled.

Astro was confused. "That's the plan?"

"We're already looking into purchasing the feather," Robotsky said.

Astro was relieved. "So you guys are completely harmless."

"NO!" Sparx protested. "We are absolutely terrifying revolutionaries."

"Who are unable to do any actual terrifying," Astro pointed out.

Sparx thought for a moment. "Yes!"

Bang!

The door to the hideout busted open. Cora stood there, holding a wrench, with the three kids behind her.

"Aargh! How did you find our secret hideout?" Sparx asked.

Cora pointed overhead. A giant neon sign read: RRF SECRET HIDEOUT. Colorful helium balloons were tied to the roof as well.

"You morons need to work on your camouflage skills," she said. She took a step toward them, tapping the wrench in her palm. "Hand over the kid or we'll rewire you and turn you into useful household appliances."

Sparx looked at Astro in amazement.

"Kid? What are you talking about? He's a—"

Astro grabbed Sparx and got into his face. "You want a piece of me, tin man?" he asked. Under his breath, he whispered, "Be cool. I'm an undercover robot from Metro City."

"I knew it," Sparx hissed back. "Viva la Robot-olution."

Astro turned back to Cora. "These guys aren't doing any harm. Let's just leave them."

Cora shrugged. "Whatever you say."

Sparx whispered in Astro's ear. "Thank you, brother. The RRF is forever in your debt."

Astro followed Cora and the others outside.

"So what *is* your name?" Cora asked.

"Um, Toby, but that's not who I really am," Astro said. "You see—"

"Dude, it's a simple question," Cora said impatiently.

"My name's . . . Astro," he replied. Those robots were goofy, but they had managed to come up with a pretty good name. "Call me Astro."

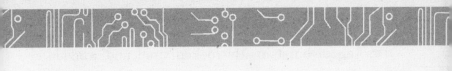

CHAPTER 11

Back in Metro City, Orrin answered the door to Dr.
Tenma's apartment. Armed soldiers pushed him out of
the way. President Stone and General Heckler marched
in. They looked angry.

"Good afternoon," Orrin said politely. "How—"

"Search the apartment!" General Heckler barked.
"Leave no stone unturned!"

Dr. Elefun stepped into the hallway, confused.

"Arrest this man!" President Stone ordered.

"Yes, sir!" General Heckler replied. He nodded, and
two soldiers grabbed Elefun by the arms. They attached
handcuffs to his wrists.

"What are you doing? Stop!" Dr. Elefun cried.

"Where is Dr. Tenma's robot son?" President Stone
asked.

"He isn't here!" Dr. Elefun said.

Dr. Tenma burst in. He looked tired and worried. "What's the meaning of this?"

"You put your core for my Peacekeeper into *your* robot," President Stone said angrily. "I'm running for reelection, in case you hadn't noticed, and we're in an arms race with the Surface!"

"An arms race," Dr. Elefun muttered. "What nonsense."

"It was my stupid mistake," Dr. Tenma said. "When I lost my son, I thought I'd be able to . . . I thought . . . "

"I hate losing, too," President Stone said. "Ask any of my wives. But we've got to get over all of this personal stuff. You're head of the Ministry of Science, Tenma. It's time to move on. Get the core back. Get it into the Peacekeeper. Let some good come from all this mess."

Dr. Tenma glanced at Dr. Elefun, still in handcuffs. His friend shouldn't have to be punished for this. He nodded in agreement.

"When you find the robot I'll deactivate it and give you the core," Tenma promised.

"Good man," President Stone said. He nodded to the soldiers. "Let him go."

The soldiers freed Dr. Elefun. He shook his head and looked out the window, at the world beyond Metro City.

"I hope you never find him," he said softly.

<hr>

Down on the Surface, Astro followed his new friends across a rickety bridge. Rope scraps connected the wood planks and pieces of metal together. It swayed as they walked. Trashcan walked behind them.

Astro looked down at the makeshift huts below. Everything was made out of old robot parts and other garbage thrown down from Metro City.

"So there are actually people living in these ruins?" he asked.

His remark made Cora angry. "Ruins? Hey, it might not look like much to a Metro City kid, but this place is home to us."

Cora stopped in front of the opening of a long, twisting tube. It looked like something from a water park ride.

"Here we are," she said.

Cora jumped in, and they all followed her, sliding down the tube. Astro bumped into Trashcan.

"Sorry," he said.

They landed in front of what looked like a big junkyard surrounded by a tall fence. The door to the gate was closed. Cora gave it a kick and lights turned on, illuminating a pattern of shapes.

A panel on the top of the door slid open and a boy

poked his head out.

"What's the password?"

"Don't make me hurt you," Cora said.

"Er . . . close enough," said the boy. "Enter."

The door opened and they pushed their way in. Astro followed cautiously. He had never seen a place like this before.

At first glance, it looked like some kind of robot repair shop, with worktables, tools, and robot parts scattered everywhere. But the place was crawling with kids, and they all looked out of control. Some of them were playing video games on busted television screens. One small boy was starting a chainsaw. A girl was juggling three sharp knives. Two boys were dueling with golf clubs. The sound of popping firecrackers filled the air.

A baseball whizzed past Astro's head. Nearby, he saw a boy shoot an apple off a kid's head with a bow and arrow.

"We're out of apples. We're on to grapes," the boy announced.

A little girl wearing patched-up clothes walked up to Cora, holding a plunger.

"Hey, Cora, did you bring me back something?" she asked.

"The perfect gift for a sweet little girl," Cora said.

She reached into her bag and pulled out a chainsaw. The little girl jumped for joy.

Cora smiled. "Enjoy."

The little girl revved the chainsaw and ran off. Soon there were screams from the other side of the junkyard.

Cora ducked as a tire swung over her head. It hit Astro, knocking him to the ground.

"Ouch," Astro said, getting to his feet.

"You need ten sets of eyes around here," Cora advised.

She headed up a ladder to the second level of the junkyard. A stout man was bent over a worktable, welding something. Astro hung back.

"Hey, Hamegg," Cora called out.

The man spun around. The blue light from the welder illuminated his face, and, for a moment, Astro thought he looked frightening. But at the sight of the kids, he smiled warmly. It changed him completely. Now he looked like a chubby, friendly man.

"Aha! Back so soon? You kids find anything good for me today?" Hamegg asked.

Astro recognized his face from the image projected on Robotsky's chest. Hamegg wore a grease-stained mechanic's jumpsuit. Astro watched him carefully. According to Sparx and the others, Hamegg was a bad guy.

Cora and the others emptied their bags on the worktable. Hamegg rifled through the items.

"I don't know, kids," he said. "A lot of dead batteries. A lot of elbows here. The knee joint of a toilet cleaning robot? I told you I need heads."

"We could have got a lot better stuff, but—" Cora began.

"Whoa!" Astro cried, interrupting her. He had been tinkering around with a broken robot in the corner. The pieces clattered to the floor.

Hamegg raised a bushy, black eyebrow. "Well, well, who do we have here?"

"His name's Astro," Zane said. "He saved us from the Scorpion Brothers."

Hamegg looked impressed. "You escaped from the Scorpion Brothers? Wow."

"Actually, I'm from Metro City," Astro told him.

"Double wow," Hamegg said. "I used to work there once upon a time."

"Really?" Astro asked.

"Why am I running a crummy body repair shop down here when I could be creating state-of-the-art robots in Metro City?" Hamegg asked.

Astro felt bad. He hadn't meant to hurt Hamegg's feelings. "Well, no, not exactly—"

"Relax, son. We're family here," Hamegg said, smiling again. "We're allowed to ask questions. The answer is: I love robots, especially the discarded ones. The more banged-up they are, the more abused, the more I like getting them back on their feet."

He plucked a tiny robot from a shelf. It flew around him with wings, like a metal mosquito.

"Oh wow!" Astro said. It was a pretty cool robot.

"It's almost a religious thing with me—kinda the way saints feel about the poor, or women feel about shoes, or fat people feel about donuts," Hamegg said dramatically. "Well, I'll stop with fat people and donuts."

Astro considered this. Hamegg seemed very sincere. And those members of the Robot Revolution Front were definitely strange. They were probably making up wild stories.

"So you're not into, er, enslaving robots?" Astro asked.

"What?" Hamegg looked genuinely surprised.

"He ran into the RRF," Cora explained.

Hamegg laughed. "I don't enslave robots, I love robots! Never forget, robots make life more abundant. They're our friends and we rely on them for our daily bread. Speaking of which, are any of you misfits hungry?"

CHAPTER 12

All of the kids in the junkyard gathered around a long table cobbled together from scraps of metal. Hamegg sat at the head.

"Let me guess—take-out pizza again?" Zane asked.

Hamegg produced some battered-looking pizza boxes.

"More like *taken out* of the trash again!" Sludge complained.

"Picky, picky," Hamegg said cheerfully. "It's only a couple of days old. Look, this one still has toppings!"

Hamegg doled out a slice to every kid at the table. Before they could dig in, he held up his hand.

"Hey! Haven't you forgotten something?" he asked.

The kids paused.

He looked at Astro. "What have they forgotten, son?"

Astro Boy

Astro thinks his name is Toby Tenma, the thirteen-year-old son of Dr. Tenma, Metro City's most celebrated scientist. What he doesn't know is that he's an advanced robot designed to look and behave like Dr. Tenma's son.

Dr. Tenma

Dr. Tenma is a scientist who has devoted his life to the invention of advanced robots. He is the creator of a great deal of the technology that has turned Metro City into such a thriving utopia.

Cora

Cora is a smart, resourceful seventeen-year-old girl who is both a tough and caring den mother to Hamegg's gang of young scavengers.

Zane, Sludge, & Widget

Cora's gang: Zane, a fourteen-year-old who is constantly trying to prove that he is a man, and Sludge and Widget, a set of trouble-making, nine-year-old twins.

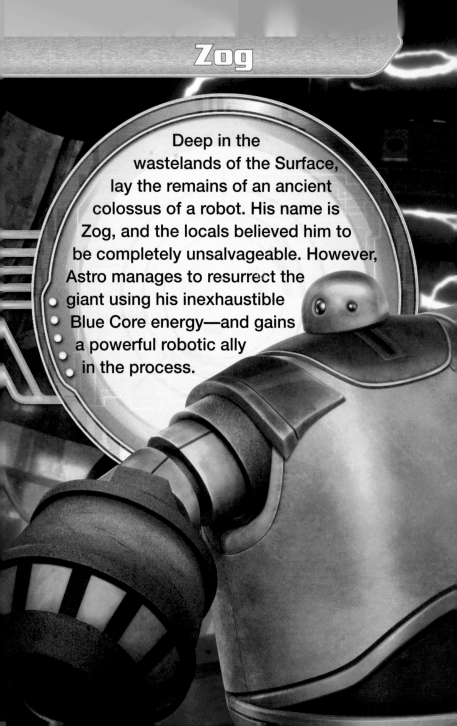

Deep in the wastelands of the Surface, lay the remains of an ancient colossus of a robot. His name is Zog, and the locals believed him to be completely unsalvageable. However, Astro manages to resurrect the giant using his inexhaustible Blue Core energy—and gains a powerful robotic ally in the process.

Dr. Elefun

Dr. Elefun is an eccentric, idealistic colleague of Dr. Tenma at the Ministry of Science. He is appalled when his invention of Blue Core energy is hijacked by the military.

Orrin

One of the first domestic robots ever built, Dr. Tenma keeps Orrin around mainly as a historical relic. When he has time to take things slow, Orrin manages to do a decent job of keeping Dr. Tenma and Astro fed and their penthouse tidy.

President Stone

President Stone is no stranger to conflict. In fact, he can find it anywhere . . . and when he can't, he is a genius at creating it.

The Peacekeeper

The Peacekeeper is a breakthrough in mad science. In addition to a frightening array of high-powered machine guns, missiles, and plasma cannons, the Peacekeeper is also equipped with prototype "adaptive technology," allowing it to absorb and control anything in its destructive path.

Hamegg

Hamegg is the strangely charismatic leader of a gang of kids who scavenges for spare parts in the robot junkyard. He was once a visionary scientist with Dr. Tenma in the Ministry of Science, but now he runs a robot repair shop down on the Surface.

Trashcan

Trashcan serves Cora and the gang as their faithful pet, friend, scout, and, of course, trash can. He may be an older model, but he's still as scrappy as a puppy.

The RRF

The Robot Revolutionary Front is a group of artificial intellectuals who spend their days pontificating about robot rights and attempting to coordinate a grand robot insurrection.

Mr. Squirt & Mr. Squeege

It's not easy keeping the thousands of windows in Metro City clean and shiny, but the Ministry of Science gets the job done with the help of specially designed, state-of-the-art robotic cleaning birds.

"Um ... grace?" Astro guessed.

"Exactly," Hamegg said. "Grace!"

The little girl whom Cora had given the chainsaw to looked up. She wore a baseball cap with the name "Grace" on it.

"What?" Grace asked.

"Turn on the TV, sweetheart, would you please?" Hamegg asked. "That's a dear."

Grace got up and turned on several television sets arranged all around the table. Each TV blared a different, loud show, a mix of professional wrestling, game shows, and car races.

"Well, Bon Appeteetee!" Hamegg said.

Everyone started eating, staring at the TV sets. Astro didn't touch his pizza. For one thing, as a robot, he didn't need to eat. But Astro wasn't sure if he would eat it if he were human. It looked pretty gross.

A scruffy kid next to him eyed his pizza slice hungrily. "Yo, new guy! You gonna eat that?" he asked.

"You can have it if you want it," Astro said, sliding his plate over.

"Thanks. I'm Sam," the kid told him.

"Don't be so nice. You're gonna starve to death," Cora warned Astro. She bit into her pizza and winced. "Or be the only survivor."

The kids laughed.

"So tell me, Astro, do your folks know where you are?" Hamegg asked.

"I don't have any parents," Astro replied.

"How very sad," Hamegg said. "Did you lose them? Or even sadder, did they lose *you*?"

Hamegg's words were too close to the truth. Astro decided he might as well be honest.

"I never really had parents," he began.

"No, the truth is I'm actually a . . . I'm a . . . " Astro was still too afraid to tell the truth.

"A *what*?" Cora asked impatiently.

Trashcan started jumping up and down behind Astro. He knew what Astro really was.

Astro looked at Cora. He wanted to tell her the truth. But what if she rejected him, just like Dr. Tenma had? He was just starting to feel comfortable here. Where else could he go?

"I'm a . . . " He just couldn't say it.

"Don't worry, son. We're all orphans down here," Hamegg interjected. "Nothing to be ashamed about."

Astro sighed with relief. "So none of you have parents?"

"Parents?" Sludge asked. "Are you kidding me?"

"This whole place is a parent-free zone," Cora explained.

Zane stuffed another slice of pizza into his mouth. "I was born in the scrap heap. I was raised by wild dogs," he bragged, with his mouth full of food.

"Really? Are you sure it wasn't wild pigs?" Cora teased.

Everyone laughed, including Zane. Astro joined in.

Maybe, just maybe, this was where he belonged.

It was really late. After dinner, the other kids got ready for bed. Astro cobbled together a cot from some old robot springs and fabric scraps. Hamegg made the rounds of the junkyard, checking on all of his charges. He stopped by Astro.

"Feeling homesick for Metro City, Astro?" Hamegg asked.

"No," Astro answered, although he wasn't sure if that was true.

Hamegg sat down on an old oil drum. "Me neither," he said. "I was head of advanced robotics at the Ministry of Science. Oh yeah, right up there with Tenma and the other muckety-mucks."

Astro was curious. Hamegg had known Toby's father. "What happened?" he asked.

"What always happens to genius," Hamegg said.

"They were intimidated by my talent, so they threw me away like an old battery."

"I'm sorry," Astro said. *He* knew what that felt like.

"Not your problem," Hamegg said. "You know, I've got a hunch about you, Astro. There's always room for a good kid in this family. Now how about getting some shut-eye? Good night . . . son."

He tucked Astro into his bed, bringing the scraps of junk up to his chin.

"Good night, Hamegg," Astro said.

Hamegg left, and Astro noticed Trashcan staring at him, his eyes glowing in the darkness.

"I'm going to tell them," Astro said. "Just not yet, okay?"

Trashcan gave Astro a look that clearly said, "You'll be sorry." Then he trotted away.

Astro didn't let it worry him. Everything would work out fine—it had to.

Then he closed his eyes and drifted off into a peaceful sleep.

CHAPTER 13

The next morning, Astro lined up with the rest of the junkyard kids. Hamegg stood by the door, patting each head as the kids filed past.

Astro stepped up with Trashcan by his side.

Hamegg smiled at Astro. "Nice to have you on the team, son. Bring me home something special. Make me proud."

"I'll try," Astro promised.

At his side, Trashcan began to beep, jumping up and down.

Beep. Beep. Beep. Beep. He wouldn't stop! Astro knew he was trying to tell Hamegg that he was a robot.

"You might need to tighten a few of his bolts," Astro suggested.

Hamegg patted Trashcan's head. "Do I have to tighten your bolts?"

Astro hurried out, glad that Hamegg hadn't caught on. The kids took off in all directions, but Cora, Zane, Widget, and Sludge stuck together. He followed them into an area he hadn't seen before. They were in some kind of meadow. There were even a few trees here and there. Broken robot parts littered the ground like bones in the desert. Huge scrap heaps loomed in the distance.

Trashcan continued to beep at Astro.

"Hey, knock it off," Astro hissed. "I'll tell them—just not yet, okay?"

Trashcan beeped some more. Then he stopped, running ahead. He stopped near Cora and started frantically digging in the dirt. Astro shook his head and caught up to Cora and Zane.

"What does Hamegg want parts for?" he asked them.

"He's a genius," Cora said proudly. "He can make cool robots from pretty much any old scrap. And then he puts them into Hamegg's Robot Games."

"Robot games?" Astro asked.

"They're a tradition down here," Cora explained. "Once a year, Hamegg puts on a big show and he always needs new performers. It's kind of a Roman thing."

"And pretty cool," Zane added.

Astro looked around the meadow. "You're not going

to find much here. It's a graveyard."

Cora raised an eyebrow. "Mr. Metro City's first day and already he's an expert."

"You'd be surprised," Astro replied. "I know a thing or two about robots."

Widget called out from up ahead. "I think we've got something!"

"See?" Cora told Astro. She raised her voice. "Coming!"

She walked right past Trashcan. The dog ran up to Astro and Zane and started beeping again, jumping up on Zane.

"Hey! What's the matter, boy?" Zane asked.

Trashcan nodded to the patch of dirt he'd been digging. He'd carved out the words "HE'S A ROBOT" in huge letters, with an arrow pointing to Astro. Astro turned pale. His secret was out!

"Whoa," Zane said. He looked at Astro, then back at Trashcan, then at Astro again.

He shrugged. "Makes me wish I could read."

He ran off after Cora. Trashcan hung his head, frustrated.

"Nice try, rust-bucket," Astro said.

He started to catch up with the others, but something caught his eye. A huge, rusting robot covered with patches of grass and weeds was lying in the clearing nearby.

"Cora, hey!" Astro called out. "I think I found something!"

Cora and the kids ran over. When they saw what Astro was pointing at, they laughed.

"Ha! That's just an old construction robot," Cora said. "It fell to the Surface a hundred years ago."

"Do you think Hamegg could use it?" Astro asked. Curious, he walked toward the big robot.

"If he had a robot like Zog, he'd make a fortune in the games," Cora said. "But it's just a piece of junk. We used to have picnics in its head."

Astro wanted to bring back something great to impress Hamegg. This robot could be just the thing.

"Give me a minute," he said.

He ran to the robot.

"It weighs hundreds of tons," Cora called out. "What are you going to do, put it in your backpack?"

She'd flip if she knew I could really carry it, Astro thought. He examined the bot. The robot's body was big and barrel-shaped—you could fit a small family inside it. Astro scooted behind some overgrown weeds, making sure the others couldn't see him. Then he peeled back a steel plate and stepped inside.

The robots circuits were covered in cobwebs, but everything looked like it was in place. Astro spotted a nameplate and wiped the dust from it. It read, "Z.O.G. Built to Last."

"Zog," Astro said out loud. "Hello, Zog."

Astro's eyes glowed, and he scanned the dusty circuits. He quickly located the power source—a dead battery.

"I know you're not dead. You're just pretending," Astro told him.

He took a deep breath and focused a beam of Blue Core energy on the battery. Nothing happened.

"Come on, big guy. Time to wake up," Astro urged.

Astro tried harder. The beam got brighter.

"Zog, let me help you . . . come on."

Slowly, the circuits began to crackle, coming to life. A blue light flickered across the control panel. Astro quickly jumped out of the robot's body.

The ground rumbled as the robot awoke from his hundred-year sleep.

Zog was alive!

○———○

Back at the junkyard, Hamegg was testing one of his robots in the outdoor courtyard. The human-sized robot was dancing around, pounding the air with his fists like a boxer in training.

"Hold it right there, Twinkle Toes," Hamegg said. "Are you some kind of ice-skater? You planning on ballroom dancing with your opponent, or you going to fight him?"

Eager to please, the robot started punching harder and delivering martial-arts style kicks in the air.

"Easy, champ, save a little for the show," Hamegg said.

The robot paused, waiting for Hamegg's approval.

"That was nice, very nice," Hamegg told him. "Kid, I think you got the makings of a champion."

The happy robot did a series of backflips across the courtyard like some crazed gymnast. He landed on both feet, raising his arms in victory.

Splat!

Zog accidentally crushed the robot with his giant foot. Astro and the kids rode in on Zog's massive shoulders. Hamegg looked up in amazement. A small, dome-shaped head sat on top of the robot's huge body. One of the robot's thick arms ended in a cement mixer.

"Sorry about your robot," Astro said.

Hamegg stared, open-mouthed, unable to talk for a minute. Then he spoke. "What? Oh him? He wasn't really working out, anyway. But hey, this guy's something else!"

The kids climbed down as Hamegg began to inspect Zog. He looked like a kid who had just unwrapped a birthday present.

"Boy, they don't make 'em like this anymore," he gushed. "Look at the legs on this baby. Look at those feet. None of your carbon fiber plastic junk on this guy. That's solid pig iron. He's even got the original detailing."

"Astro got it running, which I'm still having trouble believing," Cora said, with a suspicious glance at Astro.

Hamegg's eyes widened. "But it's been dead for at least a century!" He turned to Astro. "How did you do it? Please tell me how you did it!"

Astro shrugged. "I just kicked it, you know, like a vending machine. 'Give me back my money.' It was nothing."

"You hear that, kids? A genius with modesty," Hamegg said. "I didn't think that occurred in nature. Astro, you're almost too good to be true. Keep this up and I just may have to adopt you."

Astro beamed happily. Hamegg grabbed a handheld device from his workbench and waved it over Zog. The needle on the device jumped.

"Holy cow!" Hamegg cried. "This thing's got enough

juice to run a city."

As he talked to the kids, the device was pointing at Astro. The needle jumped even higher, and the machine began to beep frantically.

"What was that?" Astro asked.

Hamegg smacked the device.

"Oh nothing, son," he said, eyeing Astro curiously. "Just another machine with a mind of its own!"

He turned back to Zog with a gleam in his eye. Astro was feeling too happy to notice that Hamegg was suspicious of him.

I'm sure there's a place for you. You just have to find it, Dr. Elefun had told him.

Cora and the kids accepted him. Hamegg might even want to adopt him.

Maybe I've found my place at last, Astro thought.

CHAPTER 14

Astro and the others spent the rest of the day getting Zog in tip-top shape. Hamegg supervised them. They washed off the mold with a power washer—and managed to get each other wet in the process. They scraped off rust and pounded out dents. They repainted him, adding his name in red letters across his chest and spiffy rays of color on his neck and arms. They waxed and polished him until he shone.

Astro could have done the work twice as fast as everyone else, but he made sure to slow down so no one would notice he was different. Fixing Zog took hours, but every minute of it was fun for Astro. The kids laughed and joked the whole time. Astro felt really happy.

Astro and Cora climbed a ladder to add some finishing touches to Zog's face. Cora lost her balance and slipped. Astro quickly zoomed around the ladder to catch her from behind.

Cora was confused.

"How did you do that?" she asked.

"I'm faster than I look," Astro lied. She gave him a look of disbelief. "I work out."

If Astro had looked down, he would have noticed that Hamegg had seen the whole thing. The chubby man didn't let on, but inside, the wheels of his brain were churning.

Finally, Zog was finished. Hamegg, Astro, and the kids gathered in front of Zog. Hamegg set up a camera to take their photo.

"Everybody say Limburger!" Cora called out.

"Limburger!" everyone yelled. Astro laughed.

In that moment, he felt like he was part of a real family.

Soon it was time for dinner. When it got dark, Astro went outside to check on Zog. Trashcan followed at his heels.

The huge robot was snoring peacefully.

"Good night, Zog," Astro whispered.

Trashcan ran off for a second and came back, holding a rusty pipe. He dropped the pipe at Astro's feet.

"Hey, Trashcan. You wanna play? Fetch!"

Astro threw the pipe—but he forgot just how strong

he was. The pipe disappeared into the darkness.

"Oops!" Astro said. He followed Trashcan as he ran after the pipe.

They emerged into a small clearing filled with junked-out cars and other appliances. From here, Astro could see Metro City shining like a bright cloud in the distance.

He noticed Cora by herself, sitting on the ground next to one of the cars.

"Hello? Hello? Hello?" she was saying.

"Hello?" Astro answered.

Cora jumped and hit her head on the open car door. "Ouch! Hey, didn't your nanny bots tell you it's rude to sneak up on people?"

"How's your head?" Astro answered.

"It's still on," Cora said, tough as ever.

Astro saw she'd been talking to the old cell phone she'd found the day before. She started hitting buttons on it. Nothing happened. She frowned, gazing up at the sky.

"You know, they say that sometimes when it's really clear like tonight, you can still call through to Metro City," she said wistfully. She looked a little sad—not tough at all.

"You want to call Metro City?" Astro asked. Cora

hated it there.

Cora shook the sad expression off of her face. "Yeah," she said. "You never made a prank call? The only thing is—I can't get this stupid phone to work."

She tossed the cell phone in frustration, but Astro reached out and grabbed it.

"Let me try," he said.

Cora shrugged. "Knock yourself out."

Astro pressed some buttons. He put it to his ear. Then, making sure Cora couldn't see him, he zapped it with a shot of Blue Core energy. The phone lit up.

"Here," he said, handing it to Cora. "It's kind of weak, but there's a signal."

"Hey, not bad," Cora said. "The kid's got hidden talents."

"You have no idea," Astro said nervously. He didn't feel right keeping his secret from Cora. Maybe now was the time.

Cora punched in some numbers on the phone. Astro could hear a beep from the other end.

"Come on, somebody pick up," Cora said into the phone. "Please pick up. It's me, Cora."

She paused. "I miss you guys," she said softly.

Cora turned off the phone and slumped back against the car.

"Are you okay?" Astro asked.

"Sometimes I wonder if they've even noticed I'm gone," Cora replied.

"Who?" Astro asked.

Cora avoided his eyes. "My parents."

"Your parents?" Astro thought she didn't have any.

"That's right," Cora said. "Now you know the truth about me. What are you waiting for? Go tell Zane and the others. Cora's from Metro City and still trying to call home."

"Don't forget the part about being raised by nanny bots," Astro teased.

A hint of a smile broke out on Cora's face, and then it grew. He sat down beside her.

"Everybody's got secrets," he told her. "I wouldn't tell them. You can trust me."

Cora leaned against him. "I know. You're a good guy, Astro."

Astro took a deep breath. It was now or never.

"Can I tell you something?" Astro asked. "My secret?"

"Sure," Cora replied. "That's what friends are for, right?"

"Do you ever feel like you just don't fit in?" Astro asked. "Like you're different from everyone else, kind of like an outsider?"

"Of course. Everyone feels like that sometimes," she answered.

"Well, the last few days have been different for me. I mean, being with all you guys . . . and Hamegg . . . "

Astro wasn't sure how to explain things. "The thing I need to tell you is . . . I'm a rrrrrrr . . . a rrrrrr . . . "

Cora looked at him quizzically. Astro desperately wanted to tell her the truth. But he was too afraid.

"I'm rrrreally starting to like it here with you. With you guys," Astro said.

Cora snuggled a little closer to him. "Yeah, well, we like you, too, Astro."

Trashcan bounded up with the pipe in his mouth. He dropped it at their feet and wagged his tail. Then he rolled over onto his back. Cora and Astro laughed.

"I know it's not the same thing, but isn't Hamegg sort of like our dad now?" Astro asked.

"Yeah, I guess," Cora agreed.

They lingered in the clearing for awhile, gazing at the bright city in the sky.

The next morning, Hamegg rode through the makeshift town on a small hovercraft. He was dressed like a circus ringmaster in a top hat and a red coat with colorful gold swirls. He waved to the crowd like a celebrity. Some people cheered; others booed loudly.

"Buy your tickets, folks!" Hamegg shouted out like a carnival barker. "Don't miss the battle of the century! Look at this robot! No one can touch him! Those other robots are all cruisin' for a bruisin'! There's going to be oil spilt in the arena this afternoon, gallons of battery acid, electric wires ripped out, heads knocked off, hopes dashed, and strength rewarded."

Zog marched behind Hamegg. Astro, Cora, Zane, Widget, and Sludge were perched on the huge robot's shoulders.

The streets of the city were a mess of garbage, robot parts, and other trash. Three cardboard boxes suddenly stood up and walked into an alley. A muffled voice called out from under one of the boxes.

"Robot Revolutionary Front, transform!"

Two metal arms pushed out the side of each box. Then two metal legs. Finally, a head popped out of each one. It was Sparx, Robotsky, and Mike the Fridge— the RRF!

"Nice," Robotsky said, admiring their trans-formation.

"This is it, brothers!" Sparx said. "Time to put our new plan into action."

"Our new plan," Mike repeated.

"Much better than our old plan," Robotsky added.

Sparx gestured dramatically. "Bring out the secret weapon!"

Mike the Fridge took an old briefcase out from under his box. He opened the lid and a golden light shone on the three robots' faces.

"Aaaaaaah," they all said at once.

Robotsky reached in and took out a flashlight. "I've been looking for that!"

Sparx got an evil look on his face—at least, as evil a look as he could muster. Technically, he wasn't allowed to be evil.

"Viva la Robot-olution! Look out, Hamegg."

Back on the street, Hamegg motioned to Astro with a dramatic wave of his hand.

"Give him a hand, folks. The kid in the red boots. He's the one who got this killing machine back in the arena!" Hamegg said.

The crowd cheered.

"Hamegg really likes you," Cora remarked.

"I like him, too," Astro said. "What's he mean, 'killing machine?'"

"The robots fight until one of them is destroyed," Cora explained.

"What?" Astro was shocked.

"Don't worry," Cora told him. "Zog's going to crush them all."

Astro felt horrible. He didn't want to see any robots crushed. "That's really what happens at the robot games?"

"What did you expect? Rock, paper, scissors?" Cora joked.

From his perch on Zog, Astro could see the Battle-Bot Arena up ahead. The bleachers of the circular stadium were packed with residents of the Surface.

Zog just fit through the open archway leading into the stadium. A bunch of fighting robots warmed up with their trainers in a staging area just outside the battle ring. They passed by one robot that looked like a boxer with spikes on his metal fists. His manager, a gray-haired human, squirted oil into his joints and massaged his steel shoulders.

"Who's the robot?" his manager asked.

"I'm the robot!" replied the boxer.

"No mercy!" his manager cried.

"No mercy! No mercy! No mercy!" the robot chanted, jumping up and down.

Then the robot got a look at Zog—and his jaw dropped off, clattering to the ground.

Hamegg waved at all of the challengers. "Good luck

out there, nice knowin' ya."

Astro and the kids climbed down off of Zog. Astro approached Hamegg.

"I thought it was a show, not a slaughter," he said.

"They're just robots, son," Hamegg told him.

Astro was upset. "I thought you liked robots."

"I do!" Hamegg said cheerfully. "But at the end of the day, they're just junk waiting to happen. I know. Some of those more advanced ones from Metro City are programmed to smile and laugh just like us."

"Really?" Cora asked.

"Oh yeah," Hamegg told her. "Unfortunately, they don't have real emotions, which is why I have no problem doing this."

Hamegg reached for his toolkit and removed a laser device from it. He quickly zapped Astro with it.

It all happened so quickly, Astro didn't have time to react. He felt a charge of electricity surge through him.

Then everything went black.

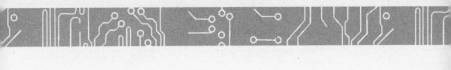

CHAPTER 15

Hamegg and the kids surrounded Astro's fallen body.

"It worked! I don't believe it," said Hamegg. He was obviously pleased with himself.

"What are you doing?" Cora asked in disbelief.

Hamegg waved the laser device in the air. "I swiped this from Dr. Tenma after he fired me from the Ministry of Science."

"Who cares?" Cora cried. "Why did you do that to Astro?"

"He's our friend!" Zane said, balling his hands into fists.

Hamegg shook his head. "I thought I raised you better. Smarter. Are you blind? He's a robot."

The kids all stared at Astro. Cora shook her head.

"It's not true. It can't be true," she said.

"Somebody programmed him to be nice," Hamegg

explained. "He's not really nice. He's just an incredibly powerful machine."

Cora still couldn't believe it. "But he was so . . ."

Hamegg put an arm around her. "I know, sweetheart. It's got to be tough."

"What are you going to do with him?" Zane asked.

Hamegg grinned. "Take a wild guess."

Nearby, the three robots disguised as cardboard boxes had witnessed the whole scene.

"Poor little comrade," Robotsky said sadly.

"Never fear, the Robot Revolutionary Front is here!" Sparx said bravely. He clutched the briefcase in his hand.

The RRF's secret weapon was about to be unleashed . . .

o————o

Astro opened his eyes, finding himself in complete darkness. He realized he was in some kind of box. He used the light from his eyes to light up the darkness. Astro saw he was dressed in a pair of black pants and a white and red shirt with a giant letter "A" on the front.

Through the box, he could hear Hamegg talking to the crowd.

"Ladies and gentlemen, boys and girls, all you riff-raff who snuck in without buying a ticket, have we got a treat for you!" he cried. "Allow me to present . . . ASTRO BOY!"

The door to the box opened, and Astro walked out into the arena, confused. Hamegg sat on a platform above him with Cora and the others. Astro looked up at Cora, but she turned away.

"I know, you're wondering what a nice-looking kid like that is doing in a place like this," Hamegg said. "That ain't no kid, folks. That's a robot from Metro City."

The crowd booed loudly.

"Astro personally told me he doesn't think much of our fighting robots. Thinks they're a bunch of sissies. Thinks you're all trailer park trash!" Hamegg said, egging them on.

"He didn't say that!" Cora protested, but nobody heard her over the boos of the crowd. They were on their feet now, shaking their fists at Astro.

"This is what we've all been waiting for!" Hamegg cried. "A fight between the Surface and Metro City. Let's get it on!"

A big Kill-Bot stomped into the ring. It had a giant spiked head and long arms with spinning saws on the end.

"Sorry, I'm not doing this," Astro said. He powered his jets and shot straight up into the open-air arena.

Zap! Some invisible force field jolted him, sending him slamming into the ground. The crowd laughed and cheered.

Groggy, Astro started to get to his feet. But the Kill-Bot loomed over him.

Pow! The bot aimed a punch at Astro. He rolled out of the way just in time.

Pow! Pow! Pow! The Kill-Bot was relentless, trying to hit Astro again and again. But Astro was too fast. Back on his feet, he powered his jets again, zipping in between the bot's deadly arms.

Astro didn't fight back. He didn't believe in hurting anybody for no good reason, not even robots. But the crowd thought he was afraid.

"Fight! Fight! Fight!" they chanted.

The Kill-Bot got angrier and angrier. He could not touch Astro. He angrily flailed his giant arms. Members of the crowd screamed and ducked.

Astro knew he had to do something. The crowd was in danger! With his superstrength, he picked up the Kill-Bot, then quickly flew up, up, into the sky.

Zap! The Kill-Bot hit the force field.

Boom! His head exploded. Metal pieces rained down on the ring.

The crowd went wild.

"Bring out the next robot!" Hamegg shouted.

A robot no bigger than Astro entered the arena. Then it quickly split up, turning into two robots. One of the robots grew until it was as tall as a tree, with spiked clubs for arms. The other robot transformed into a mass of cannons.

Bam! Bam! Astro flew out of the way. He still didn't want to fight.

He flew behind one of the robots and tapped on its shoulder.

"Hey, fella," Astro said, trying to make friends.

The startled robot fired shot after shot at Astro, trying to destroy him. Astro dodged the blasts. One of them hit the second robot, and the second robot fired back. Now the two robots were destroying each other!

Astro used his superstrength and picked one up in each hand and smacked them together. The fight was over. Hamegg's face turned purple with rage.

"Get him!" he bellowed.

Astro barely had time to regain his strength before Hamegg sent out a small army of robots. The crowd started to cheer for Astro as he took them down one by one. With the crowd distracted, the RRF put their plan into action.

Their new secret weapon wasn't a feather—it

was a feather duster!

"The secret weapon!" Sparx announced.

A jet of flame from the arena shot toward them, turning the feather duster into a pile of ashes.

"All right, go to plan B," Sparx instructed.

"What is plan B?" asked Mike.

"We all run around waving our hands in the air and screaming like little girls," Robotsky said.

"Aaaaaaaaaah!" The three robots ran and screamed.

In the ring, Astro battled challenger after challenger. He took down robots that breathed fire, robots with chainsaws for hands, and robots that spit out ninja throwing stars. The more Astro fought, the more the crowd loved him.

Finally, it looked like there were no more challengers. He gazed up at the platform, exhausted. How could Hamegg have betrayed him like this? And Cora had acted like she hated him. His dreams of joining the junkyard family were over. What would happen to him now?

But Hamegg had one more surprise in store.

"And now—the final challenger. A robot so fearsome, so powerful, even I'm afraid to watch," he announced. "Behold!"

A loud, mechanical roar shook the arena. Everyone

looked to a metal gate. The next challenger waited there, and it sounded terrifying.

The metal gate opened up, and the crowd gasped in fear. Zog was *huge!*

"I give you, the mighty Zog!" Hamegg said dramatically. "Let's see how Astro Boy does against a robot powered with the same energy he's got."

How could Hamegg do this? Astro wondered. Zog wasn't just another challenger—he was Astro's friend.

"I'm not fighting you, Zog," Astro said.

Zog took a mighty step toward Astro.

"I mean it," Astro said. "I won't fight."

Zog took another step. He was close enough now to crush him with one move of his foot. Astro looked up at him, not moving. He wasn't going to attack Zog, no matter what.

Zog reached out with one huge hand . . . and affectionately ruffled Astro's hair. The crowd laughed.

Hamegg was annoyed. "Great! A love-in. Some big finale."

He aimed a laser device and hit the button. A jolt of electricity hit Zog. The big robot writhed in pain.

"Fight! That's an order."

But Zog wouldn't do it. Hamegg zapped him again

and again. Zog was clearly hurting. He started to smoke and overheat.

But he wouldn't give in. Astro was his friend, too.

Frustrated, Hamegg aimed the laser at Astro next. Astro gasped in pain and fell down on one knee.

The crowd roared in protest. They loved Astro now.

Cora stood up. "That's enough!" she angrily told Hamegg.

"What's the matter with you?" Hamegg asked. "They're just machines. They'll do what I tell them."

Hamegg was furious now. He jumped off the platform and stormed across the field, brandishing the laser.

"What? I'm going to be embarrassed by some souped-up hotshot from Metro City? A hundred-year-old bulldozer from New Jersey? I'm turning you both off," he threatened.

Zog stomped his giant foot, shaking the ground. A huge crack opened up in the arena floor beneath Hamegg. It knocked him to the ground, and his laser device went flying.

Zog stomped toward Hamegg. He raised one giant foot, ready to crush him.

"Stop! The laws of robotics!" Hamegg yelled. "You can't hurt a human! It's been that way for fifty years."

But Zog had been built long before the laws of robotics were in place, and he knew it. For the first time in a century, he spoke.

"I'm old school," he said in a booming voice.

The members of the RRF watched in amazement from the sidelines.

"We've got to get that guy!" Sparx quipped.

The crowd froze. Was this really the end of Hamegg? Zog's foot slowly came down . . .

. . . and Astro flew underneath it, holding it up.

He didn't want to see *anyone* get hurt—even a creep like Hamegg.

Hamegg rolled out of the way. He stared up at Astro, terrified and stunned.

"What kind of robot are you?" he asked.

But Astro wasn't looking at him. His eyes were on the sky, where a military aircraft was about to descend into the arena.

President Stone had found him!

CHAPTER 16

The gunship landed in the middle of the arena. A swarm of heavily-armed soldiers emerged from the craft. They charged toward Astro with their guns raised.

Cora sprinted onto the field and picked up Hamegg's laser device. More kids and members of the crowd were hopping over the barricades. They all wanted to help Astro.

General Heckler and President Stone marched up between the soldiers. "Seize the rogue robot and secure the area!" Stone commanded.

A mass of soldiers jumped on Astro, piling on top of him like they were football players and Astro held the ball. One of Astro's red boots stuck out of the pile.

The crowd roared in protest and started to advance toward the soldiers. The standing soldiers turned their guns on them.

Back on his feet, Hamegg stared at President Stone in amazement. "Dufus? Dufus Stone? Is that you?" he asked.

President Stone froze. The crowd hissed as Hamegg walked up to him.

"It's me, Hamegg! We were in the third grade together. I used to do your homework for you, remember?" Hamegg asked.

"I've never seen you before in my life," President Stone said, but it was clear he was lying.

The crowd was throwing things at Hamegg now.

"Take me back to Metro City with you," Hamegg pleaded. "I'm begging you, Dufus. They're going to tear me limb from limb."

Two soldiers grabbed Hamegg.

"You can't call the president Dufus," one of them warned.

They dragged him away.

"He's the *president*?" Hamegg cried out in disbelief. "Yeah, pull the other one. I used to forge his report cards for him."

President Stone sidled up to General Heckler. "You told me you'd arrested everybody I went to school with," he said under his breath.

"We went all the way back to preschool, Mr.

President," Heckler assured him. "I don't know how this one slipped through the cracks."

Two soldiers pulled Astro out from under the pile-up. They gripped his arms tightly. Astro didn't even look at them. He gazed up at the clouds floating around Metro City. He remembered the first day he learned to fly. He had felt so happy, so free.

But that life was never meant to be. Dr. Elefun was wrong when he said Astro would find his place. First Metro City had rejected him, and then his friends on the Surface had, too.

Zog bellowed in rage as the soldiers dragged Astro away. He snatched up two of them like they were dolls and angrily shook them like he was about to smash their faces together.

"No, Zog! Put them down," Astro cried. He hung his head sadly. "It doesn't matter anymore."

Zog reluctantly placed the two terrified soldiers on the ground. They grabbed Astro and dragged him into the waiting aircraft.

"Time to come home," President Stone said smugly.

Inside the plane, they bound Astro's hands and feet with metal restraints. Astro gazed out the window. He could see Cora and the kids running across the arena as the plane zoomed away.

The Metro City news blared from a TV inside the plane's cabin. A female reporter with a helmet of perfect hair was talking into the camera.

"President Stone's approval rating reached a new low today when he failed to show up for a nationally televised debate with Bob Logan, the man many pundits are picking as the next president of Metro City," she reported.

The picture switched to an image of a handsome younger man waving at a cheering crowd. President Stone muted the sound on the set.

"No dirty hippie's going to sit in my Oval Office eating mung beans and stinking of patchouli oil," he said. "I've got the Blue Core and the Peacekeeper's going to start a war with the Surface. That's *bound* to get me reelected."

He offered a can of oil to Astro. The soldiers laughed.

"Why the long face, robot boy?" the president asked. "We're taking you home to your dad. Care for a drink?"

Astro didn't answer. He gazed out the window for the rest of the trip. The soldiers brought Astro directly to the Ministry of Science. Astro saw Dr. Tenma and Dr. Elefun waiting for them in Tenma's lab.

President Stone marched up to the two scientists.

"The experiment is over," he said firmly. "I want the Blue Core removed and transferred into the Peacekeeper now."

Dr Tenma turned to his friend. "Will you help me, Elefun?"

"This is where we created him," Dr. Elefun responded sadly.

The soldiers released Astro, and the president shoved him forward.

"Well, un-create him. Unplug him. It's a matter of national security," he ordered.

"Let me talk to him first," Dr. Elefun said.

Stone rolled his eyes. Dr. Elefun walked up to Astro.

"Hello, Dr. Elefun," Astro said.

"Hello, Toby."

"You look tired," Astro told the scientist. "Are you okay?"

"Not really," Dr. Elefun admitted. "This isn't your fault, you know. You're fantastic . . . superb . . . wonderful."

"Thank you," Astro said. "You know, I tried to find my place in the world. I thought I had found it . . . but fitting in can be a lot more complicated than it seems."

Dr. Elefun nodded in agreement. "Dear boy, if you only knew."

"I think maybe this is what's supposed to happen," Astro said bravely. "This is my destiny."

Tears welled up in Dr. Elefun's eyes. The president groaned in frustration.

"Boo hoo!" President Stone said meanly. "It's a MACHINE! Come on, let's get moving, people."

A soldier put a hand on Dr. Elefun's shoulder to move him away.

"This is wrong, Tenma. You know it!"

Dr. Tenma looked unsure for a moment. Then he shook his head.

"The president is right. It's just a machine," he said.

Astro looked at Dr. Elefun. "Good-bye," he said.

The scientist wiped away a tear. He watched, helpless, as the soldiers led Astro away.

They placed Astro on the same table where Dr. Tenma had brought him to life. The lifeless Peacekeeper loomed over the lab, waiting for the power inside Astro.

Dr. Tenma pressed a few buttons, and three holographic screens appeared over the table. President Stone looked eagerly at his robot war machine.

"Load the Blue Core into the Peacekeeper," he said impatiently. "I've got a press conference in ten minutes."

Tenma locked some cables into Astro's body. The

holographic screens began to register Astro's pulse—the beat of the energy flowing through his body.

Thump . . . thump . . . thump . . .

Dr. Tenma opened Astro's chest compartment. He removed the Blue Core. Astro's pulse slowed down.

. . . thump . . .

The scientist looked into Astro's eyes.

"I'm sorry," he said sincerely.

Astro smiled weakly. "Don't be," he said. "I'm sorry I couldn't have been a better Toby for you . . . Dad."

Astro's eyes closed. The thumping of his pulse faded into silence.

Dr. Tenma fell to his knees, crying.

"Well, Tenma? Is it done?" the president asked.

Tenma mustered his strength. He stood up and carried the Blue Core over to President Stone.

"It's done," Dr. Tenma said sadly.

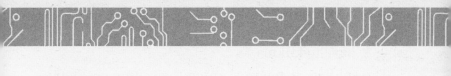

CHAPTER 17

Dr. Tenma handed the Blue Core to President Stone, who greedily accepted it. He squeezed it and leaned in close to Tenma.

"Good man," he said. "When I'm reelected, you can have the funding to make as many little toys as you want."

Dr. Tenma's heart was heavy—and then something clicked inside him. As Stone turned to walk away, he grabbed the hand holding the Blue Core.

"No!" Dr. Tenma cried.

The soldiers all turned their guns on him. He didn't flinch.

"You'll have to kill me, then," he said.

President Stone tried to yank away from Tenma's grasp. The Blue Core dropped and Dr. Elefun dove in, catching it. He turned to his friend, pleading.

"Tenma, no!" he said. "I created the Core. They're

going to have to kill me."

The soldiers listened, turning their guns on Elefun now.

"I think Metro City can learn to cope without you," Stone said dryly. "Hand it over."

Dr. Elefun opened one hand. It was empty. He opened the other. That was empty, too.

President Stone realized something was wrong.

"Tenma . . ."

The scientists had fooled him. Dr. Tenma had secretly taken the core from Dr. Elefun. Now Tenma was back at the table with Astro's body. He had lowered a protective shield around them.

Furious, the president pounded on the glass.

"Tenma! Open this. OPEN IT!"

Dr. Tenma pulled the Blue Core from his coat. Stone's face flushed with anger.

"TENMA!" he screamed.

Dr. Tenma put the Blue Core back into Astro's chest. He looked up at the hologram monitors for any signs of life.

President Stone pointed a gun at Dr. Elefun. "Open that door."

"Never," Elefun said firmly.

"I said open the door—now," the president ordered.

He pressed the gun into Elefun's chest. It hit something hard. Stone pushed Elefun's lab coat aside to reveal the scientist's security key card. He yanked it off of Elefun's neck.

"If you want something done, you gotta do it yourself," Stone said.

On the other side of the shield, the hologram screen started to show the *thump, thump, thump* of Astro's pulse. Tears of joy welled up in Tenma's eyes.

Astro was alive again!

Astro opened his eyes. "Dad, what are you doing?"

Before Tenma could reply, the shield came up. President Stone and the soldiers advanced toward them.

"Listen," Dr. Tenma told Astro. "You may not be Toby, but you're still my son."

Astro was overcome with happiness. "Thanks— Dad."

Tenma and Astro hugged.

"Hold it!" President Stone barked.

"Now! Fly!" Dr. Tenma urged Astro.

The soldiers lunged. Astro's jets powered up, and he flew across the lab. He crashed right through the window, flying outside. The window shattered into millions of tiny pieces.

"Woo-hoo!" Dr. Elefun cheered.

General Heckler found himself cheering, too. "Yes!"

"Good man, Tenma!" Dr. Elefun cried happily.

President Stone was outraged. "No!" he yelled at General Heckler. "Arrest them immediately! I want them shot for treason."

He stormed over to the Peacekeeper.

"We're going to have to use the Peacekeeper to get the Blue Core back," he said.

"Don't use the Red Core—the negative energy," Dr. Elefun begged. "We don't know how it'll behave."

"Doctor, in any conflict between positive and negative energy, the negative always prevails," the president said. "Look at human history. Look at me!"

"My point exactly," Elefun muttered.

Stone grabbed one of the scientists in the room. She held the master controls for the Peacekeeper.

"Turn this thing on," he demanded.

"I won't," the scientist said firmly.

"I have fifty reporters waiting for me outside!" he fumed. "Turn it on!"

"You don't understand the technology," Dr. Elefun said, wringing his hands.

"Ha! Technology! Who cares about it?" Stone fumed. "Who understands it? It's a robot. It'll do what I say!"

He grabbed the core with his bare hands and shoved it into the Peacekeeper's chest. The Peacekeeper came to life, its eyes glowing red.

"Red Core loaded," the Peacekeeper reported.

President Stone smiled, pleased. "You ready to do as you're told?" he asked. "You ready to rock and roll?"

"Sir!" the Peacekeeper replied, like a good soldier.

"Destroy the boy robot and bring back the Blue Core," President Stone commanded.

The Peacekeeper didn't move.

"What are you, deaf?" Stone asked angrily. "I told you to destroy the boy robot!"

The Peacekeeper descended on President Stone, absorbing the man into his steel body. The robot's eyes flashed red with anger. He spoke again—and this time, it was with the distorted, frightening voice of President Stone.

"Bring back the Blue Core!" he roared.

The scientists watched in horror. President Stone and the Peacekeeper had melded together. Their president was a terrifying, giant robot!

"Everybody out. Now!" Dr. Elefun yelled.

CHAPTER 18

Outside the Ministry of Science, a small group of reporters sat patiently in folding chairs, waiting for the press conference President Stone had promised. One of the president's aides walked up to the microphone in front of them.

"I'm sorry, guys," he apologized. "I'm getting word that President Stone may be slightly delayed."

Suddenly, Peacekeeper Stone smashed through the doorway. The reporters gasped in shock. Their president was a twenty-five-foot-tall monster!

Stone tapped the microphone. "Is this thing on?"

Terrified, the reporters screamed and ran, knocking over chairs in their panic.

"What? What are you doing? Come back!" Stone demanded.

He stomped after them. Everything he came into

contact with was absorbed by his huge body—cars, buildings, billboards, telephone poles—it didn't matter how large. Stone grew bigger and bigger every minute.

Eight small aircrafts equipped with missile launchers zoomed down from the sky and advanced on Peacekeeper Stone. His eyes flashed.

"Let's rock and roll!"

○———○

Astro flew off, unaware that Peacekeeper Stone was attacking Metro City. He was happy to be alive. His only thought was to try to escape the president's soldiers.

As he soared past a cloud, he heard a familiar squawking up ahead. Mr. Squirt and Mr. Squeegee were lazily flying in front of him.

"This is the life, buddy," Mr. Squirt said to Mr. Squeegee. "Smooth sailing."

Astro zipped past them so fast, they began to somersault in the air.

"Whoa!" they cried.

"Sorry, guys," Astro said, circling back to meet them.

"Oh no!" said Mr. Squirt. "It's that crazy kid who tried to mug us."

"I didn't try to mug you and I'm not a kid," Astro said. "I'm a robot just like you guys. What are you doing all the way out here?"

"We got tired of the rat race," Mr. Squirt answered. "We dropped out."

"We're trying to live more natural, you know, like real birds," Mr. Squeegee added.

Boom! Boom! Boom! The sound of the explosions in Metro City reached them.

"What's that?" Astro asked.

"New Year's? The Playoffs? Mother's Day?" Mr. Squirt guessed. "You know what humans are like."

Astro focused his robot vision on the city. He could see the smoke and explosions. This was no celebration. Something was wrong—and he was sure President Stone had something to do with it.

"We've got to do something," he said.

"What? About the humans?" Mr. Squirt asked. "We're robots. It's not our problem."

"Yeah, forget about them," Mr. Squeegee agreed. "What did they ever do for us?"

Boom! Boom! Astro frowned as more explosions rocked Metro City.

"Sorry, guys," he told the robots. "I've got to go help."

Astro took off with such immense velocity and force that in seconds he looked just like a burning dot speeding back to Metro City.

"He's right," Mr. Squeegee said. "According to the rules of robotics, we gotta go help."

○———————○

Astro quickly reached Metro City and tried to figure out what was going on. He flew past a digital billboard stating that the downtown area was closed off. He landed below the sign. Whatever the trouble was, it was probably close by.

A giant shadow loomed over the area. Car alarms started going off like crazy. President Stone's voice bounced off of the buildings.

"Come out, come out, wherever you are!" Stone called out.

Astro realized that President Stone and the Peacekeeper had somehow combined. The robot was as tall as a skyscraper now. It stomped around the corner. It smashed a building with a giant robot hand.

"Where are you, robot boy?" Peacekeeper Stone bellowed.

Then Stone spotted Astro. "Oh . . . hello."

Astro quickly flew off. Peacekeeper Stone stomped after him, destroying cars and buildings as he went.

Astro's eyes turned red. A message flashed across his eyes.

Activate Arm Cannons.

Astro was confused. He didn't know that Dr. Tenma had equipped him with some of the best defensive technology available.

Suddenly, his arms began to change shape. He cried out, surprised. His arms had converted into cannons!

"Cool!" Astro said.

Before he could fire . . . *Bam!* Peacekeeper Stone launched a missile at Astro, sending him hurtling through the air.

○———○

Back on the Surface, Cora, Zane, Widget, and Sludge gazed up at Metro City. They could see the smoke and hear the explosions.

"That has to be Astro," said Widget.

"I don't care if he is a robot. We've got to help him," said Sludge.

"I hear you," Zane agreed.

Behind them, Hamegg was starting up his flying car, the one he used to parade to the battle arena. Cora ran to stop him and the others followed.

Hamegg frowned when he saw Cora.

"What do you want, an apology?" he asked.

"No," Cora said. "Just the car."

"I would love to help you, but—"

Bam! Zog marched up and yanked Hamegg out of

the driver's seat.

"Bad egg," Zog said.

Cora jumped in the craft and grinned. "Anyone want to go for a ride?"

<hr />

From a street near the Ministry of Science, Dr. Tenma and Dr. Elefun watched the battle.

"He mustn't get near the Red Core," Dr. Elefun said nervously.

"Orrin, get the car," Dr. Tenma ordered.

Orrin quickly walked away. They had to help Master Toby!

Downtown, Astro slammed backward into a building. He recovered quickly, blasting the Peacekeeper with his cannons. The Peacekeeper roared as the blasts hit him, but they didn't stop him. He loomed over Astro now. He angrily swatted at Astro with his enormous hand.

The Peacekeeper lifted up his hand, expecting to find Astro underneath. But there was nothing there.

"Huh?" the Peacekeeper was confused.

Astro had escaped by drilling underground. He burst up through the ground behind the Peacekeeper. He flew up and grabbed the robot by one of his big arms. Then he pulled with all of his might.

Straining and groaning, he flipped the Peacekeeper, slamming him into the ground.

Astro grinned. He'd done it! The Peacekeeper was out cold.

But the robot wasn't down yet. He slowly rose up, absorbing all of the buildings around him. Peacekeeper Stone was beyond huge now.

"Destroy the boy robot! Must obtain the Blue Core!" Peacekeeper Stone roared.

Astro fired his cannons at full blast. The Peacekeeper screamed and angrily punched the building next to him. It broke in half.

But his anger worked against him. The broken building toppled over him. He lay underneath the rubble, completely still.

People cautiously emerged onto the streets, cheering. It looked like the Peacekeeper was really defeated this time!

Astro took a bow. "Thank you. Any time you need me."

Bam! The Peacekeeper reached out and grabbed Astro in his hand. Astro struggled to escape from the grip. Suddenly, two more hidden weapons came to Astro's aid. He shot two cannon blasts—from his butt!

The blasts hit the Peacekeeper. He let go of Astro

and fell onto the street. Astro retracted his weapons and shook his head, slightly embarrassed.

"I've got machine guns in my butt? You've got to be kidding," he said.

The Peacekeeper jumped back to his feet. He uprooted a skyscraper and swung it like a baseball bat.

Whack! He hit Astro, sending him careening into another skyscraper. Astro fell to the ground like a rock. People ran screaming out of his way.

"Look out! Run!"

The earth shook as the Peacekeeper pounded toward Astro.

"Destroy the boy robot! Obtain the Blue Core!"

He rose one enormous foot, ready to stomp Astro. Astro was still knocked out cold. He couldn't move.

Then suddenly . . . *whoosh!* Cora and the kids zipped up in Hamegg's hover car. Cora pulled Astro into the car.

They sped away just as the Peacekeeper's foot came crashing down.

CHAPTER 19

Astro slowly opened his eyes. He was in some kind of flying car. He saw Cora leaning over him. Zane, Widget, and Sludge sat next to her.

"Astro, are you hurt?" she asked.

"Yeah," Astro said, groaning.

"Where?" Cora asked.

"Everywhere," Astro replied. "Hey, who's driving?"

The kids all looked at the front seat. Trashcan was at the steering wheel.

"Aaaaaaaah!" they yelled.

Peacekeeper Stone stomped after them. He knocked down buildings in his path as easily as if they were a child's blocks.

"Trashcan, faster!" Astro urged.

Zane slipped into the driver's seat and took the controls from Trashcan. Cora and Astro hugged each other as the Peacekeeper got closer and closer.

Boom! Boom! Boom!

Transformers around the city exploded as the power went out. The whole city was silent for a moment. Then, suddenly, all of Metro City violently lurched sideways. The Peacekeeper screamed as he fell over, crashing into the ground.

Zane was confused. "Why are we going up?" he asked.

"No, the city's going down!" Cora yelled.

Astro realized what was happening. Without power, the technology that kept Metro City magically hovering over the Surface had failed. If he didn't do something, the city would be destroyed!

"I have to take care of this," Astro said. Every inch of him hurt, but he pushed the pain away. He powered his jets and zoomed from the car.

"Astro, no!" Cora yelled.

The kids were safe in their hover car. Zane steered them away. Astro flew down past the falling city. He gripped the edge of the city with all his might, trying to keep it from crashing to the surface. He focused every ounce of energy he had.

People fell out of windows. Cars skidded down the street. Astro pushed harder. He had to straighten things out before anyone fell off!

"Aaaaaaagh!" Astro groaned.

He felt himself weakening.

I can't hold on anymore! Astro thought.

Then, just when he was about to collapse, the city leveled out and landed on the Surface. He let go, sighing with relief.

Up above him, Peacekeeper Stone emerged from the smoking bubble. Down below him, he heard a voice.

"Oy, ugly!"

The Peacekeeper looked around.

"Down here!"

The voice came from Sparx, who stood next to Robotsky and Mike. Sparx was shaking his fist.

"We, the Robot Revolutionary Front, demand immediately that you cease oppressing our comrade, Astro," Sparx said. "And we would like to remind you that while the laws of robotics state that we are unable to harm a human, there is nothing to say we can't do some serious damage to a monster. Right, comrades?"

There was no reply. Sparx turned around and saw Robotsky and Mike running away, terrified.

"This isn't how we voted!" Sparx called after them.

"Where are you, robot boy?" Peacekeeper Stone shouted. "I know you're still alive."

Astro flew up behind him, holding a giant metal girder.

Peacekeeper Stone continued, "You can't hide from—"

Slam! Astro hit the robot over the head with the girder.

"Aaaaaah!" Peacekeeper Stone cried. He shook his head, spitting out a metal tooth.

"Is that all you got?" he challenged.

Astro tossed the girder aside and cracked his knuckles. He was ready for action. With a roar, he zoomed toward Peacekeeper Stone, pummeling the giant robot's metal chest like a boxer hitting a speed bag.

Then the big robot's chest opened wide, and a mechanical claw grabbed Astro in an iron grip.

"Objective complete. Blue Core obtained," Peacekeeper Stone announced.

He started to pull Astro inside his body, where the Red Core glowed brightly. Astro's eyes flashed red in warning. Just as he was about to be absorbed by the Peacekeeper, there was a huge flash and an explosion.

Astro went flying backward, landing on the top floor of a skyscraper. Peacekeeper Stone fell to the ground in agony.

"Toby!"

Astro turned to see that his father had found him.

"Dad?" Astro ran to Dr. Tenma and fell into his arms with relief. But something was worrying him.

"I don't understand. Why didn't it absorb me?" he asked.

"Because it can't." Tenma replied. "If the Red and the Blue Core come together . . . well, you both die."

Astro gazed out across the city. The Peacekeeper was back on his feet. Cora and the kids were zipping between the buildings, searching for Astro. Peacekeeper Stone spotted the vehicle and grabbed it in his hand.

Astro knew what he had to do. It was all very clear to him now.

"This is it. This is what I was created for," Astro said. "This is my destiny."

"Toby, NO," Dr. Tenma said sternly. He had lost his son twice already. He wasn't about to lose him again.

"I'm sorry, but that isn't my name anymore," Astro said. "Good-bye, Dad."

Astro's face darkened. His eyes glowed with determination. Then he launched himself right at the Peacekeeper.

"No!" Dr. Tenma yelled.

Cora and the kids gasped in amazement as Astro streaked toward the immense robot. Sensing danger,

Peacekeeper Stone stepped backward and swatted at Astro.

Astro didn't hesitate. He flew straight for the Peacekeeper's chest.

Once the Red and Blue Cores met, they both would be destroyed.

It was the only way.

CHAPTER 20

Startled, Peacekeeper Stone lost his grip on the hover car. Zane sped away, then circled back around. The Peacekeeper was frantically clawing at the hole Astro had made in his chest. But he was too late.

Boom!

The Peacekeeper exploded, spewing forth everything he had absorbed during his rampage—even President Stone. The dazed man tumbled to the ground.

President Stone stood up in the rubble, brushing off his black uniform. "What happened? Where am I? Who am I?"

Nobody paid attention to him. Everyone rushed to Astro's fallen body. It had broken apart into pieces.

Cora gently arranged the pieces together, her eyes filling with tears.

"Who is he?" a man in the crowd asked.

"I don't know, but he saved us," a woman said. "That robot saved the whole city."

"Why would he care?" the man wondered.

Dr. Elefun pushed his way forward. "Because that robot had more humanity than most of us," he said. He looked at Cora. "Who are you?"

"I'm a friend of his from the Surface," Cora said.

"You're from the Surface?" someone asked.

The crowd murmured in surprise. President Stone had always told them that Surface dwellers were violent savages. But Cora and the kids looked perfectly nice.

"Can you fix him?" the man in the crowd asked.

"No, I'm afraid not," Dr. Elefun said.

"Then can you make another one like him?" asked the woman.

"No. His Blue Core was unique," Dr. Elefun replied. "It could have regenerated the earth, brought back the forests, healed the planet. Now it's died with him."

"It's not fair," Cora said tearfully. "All he ever did was help people."

"Not just people," Zog said.

Cora nodded. "Astro brought Zog back to life."

Dr. Elefun raised an eyebrow. "How?"

"The blue stuff," Zog replied.

The scientist's eyes lit up. "Do you have any of that blue stuff left?"

Zog nodded.

"Do you think you could spare some for our friend here?" Elefun asked.

Zog stepped forward and picked up Astro. He beamed a ray of Blue Core energy with his eyes into Astro's lifeless body. Everyone waited, holding their breath.

Astro's eyes fluttered open.

"Thank you, Zog," he said. He hugged the big robot's finger.

"No biggie," Zog said.

Astro sat up. "Dr. Elefun? Cora? What happened? Is the Peacekeeper gone?"

Dr. Elefun smiled. "Astro, I think you've finally found your place in the world. You're a hero. A robot with the heart of a lion, and people finally know it."

The crowd cheered wildly. They lifted Astro up, carrying him through the streets of Metro City.

"This is your destiny!" Dr. Elefun called to him.

A very confused President Stone wandered through the crowd.

"Where am I? Who am I?" he asked angrily. "These are simple questions and I want some answers!"

A group of soldiers surrounded him.

"You're President Stone, sir," a soldier told him. "And I'm afraid you're under arrest."

Two soldiers grabbed his arms. Two others dragged General Heckler with them.

"The president, you say?" Stone asked. "That sounds pretty decent. Am I a good president?"

"History will judge, sir," the soldier replied.

In another part of the crowd, Sparx, Robotsky, and Mike were trying to recruit Zog to their cause.

"A robot who's actually allowed to harm humans," Sparx marveled. "You're a perfect fit for our organization!"

"Humans made me the robot I am today," Zog said. "Why would I want to hurt them?"

"I never thought about it like that before," Sparx admitted.

"How about joining just for the camaraderie?" Robotsky asked. "We have slogan-chanting practice on weekends. Chess night. We play charades."

"What about knitting?" Zog asked. "I like to knit."

Sparx looked at the others. They nodded.

"We could do knitting," Sparx said.

Dr. Tenma stood by his car next to Orrin. They watched the parade of people carry Astro victoriously down the street.

"That young robot's my son, you know," Tenma said proudly.

"Yes, Master," Orrin agreed.

"I don't want you to call me master anymore, Orrin," Tenma said. "In fact, take the day off. Go on, enjoy yourself with the robot ladies and so forth."

Orrin beamed. "Thank you Mast—uh, Dr. Tenma."

"Call me Bill," Tenma said.

Orrin smiled and rolled away. "Phew! I am so freaked right now."

He joined the parade of people carrying Astro. Other robots were celebrating, too. It was the first time in Metro City that humans and robots had come together as equals.

A news crew appeared. They filmed Astro being carried through the city. Cora walked closely beside him.

"This is Geraldo Segunda for OmniNews Network," the reporter said, putting a microphone in Cora's face. "Can we have a few words for the viewers at home?"

Before Cora could answer, her cell phone rang. She took it out of her pocket.

"Hello?"

Her face lit up. "Mom? Dad?"

She listened for a moment, blinking back tears. "You

and Dad have been looking for me on the Surface?"

She put her hand over the phone and signaled to Astro.

"It's my folks. They're watching us on TV!" she said excitedly. She spoke back into the phone. "Of course I know Astro. He's my friend."

Cora listened and rolled her eyes. "Of course, I realize he's a robot, Dad." She smiled as she heard his reply. "Oh good, you like robots now."

Astro smiled and waved at the crowd. He spotted Dr. Tenma on the sidelines. Astro waved. Tenma waved back.

"Who's that?" Cora asked.

"My dad," Astro said proudly.

"Your dad?" Cora asked. How could a robot have a dad?

Astro shrugged. "It's a long story."

Suddenly, sirens blared throughout the city. Soldiers rushed in. Astro tensed. Was the Peacekeeper back?

"Everyone take cover!" one of the soldiers yelled. "There's an alien threat approaching Earth!"

Astro looked up. A huge creature with slimy tentacles covered the sky.

People screamed and ran in terror. Astro powered up his jets.

"Wait!" Dr. Elefun called out. "Are you sure you're ready for this, Astro?"

Astro nodded. Dr. Elefun was right. This was his destiny—to be a hero.

"I was made ready," Astro replied as he blasted off into the sky.